William Averitt

Stories and Poems of western Texas

William Averitt

Stories and Poems of western Texas

ISBN/EAN: 9783337407193

Printed in Europe, USA, Canada, Australia, Japan

Cover: Foto ©Andreas Hilbeck / pixelio.de

More available books at **www.hansebooks.com**

STORIES AND POEMS OF

WESTERN TEXAS

BY

WILLIAM AVERITT

———

NEW YORK
JOHN B. ALDEN, PUBLISHER
1890

PREFACE.

FOR several years, and while at various occupations, I have been in the habit of writing either a story or poem on some striking occurrence or mode of life of Western Texas, always attempting to give a faithful delineation of life, whether attractive or not; and I have now mustered up the courage to issue a few of these in this small volume.

So far as I know, but few things have been written about the country, which these stories attempt to describe, by native writers. Nearly all of these stories I have read were written by authors unacquainted with the people or the land of which they wrote. And to this is due, to a great extent, the erroneous impression entertained abroad concerning our country. These writers describe the inhabitants as uncultivated, lawless semi-barbarians. This belief has become so deeply rooted in even the bordering states, that it seems futile to attempt to claim anything like civilization or excellence for this country. Such may be taken as praise springing from undue patriotism, although all know that this country is settled by people from all the most enlightened nations of the globe.

Whatever may be the merits or defects of these productions, I hope that they will be read with indulgence proportionate to the sincere intentions with which they are issued.

WILLIAM AVERITT.

COLEMAN, TEXAS.

March, 1890.

CONTENTS.

STORIES AND POEMS OF WESTERN TEXAS.

A BLIZZARD.

THE sky is clear, and not the slightest breeze
   Disturbs the perfect stillness of the air;
And the gray branches of the naked trees
   Are bathed in warmth of almost summer glare;
And the buds swell in the unnatural ease.

The wild geese clamor in their restless flight
   On to a region of perpetual spring,
A dusky vapor brings precocious night;
   Cold marble clouds float up, foreshadowing
The dreaded wind-storm coming in its might.

First comes a gentle puff of wind that feels
   Like freezing water thrown against the cheek—
Precursor of the boisterous wave that wheels
   The bluish haze around the cliff and peak,
And strikes the woods, and roars like thunder-peals.

The winds blow through the night with painful
     sound,
   Pierce heartlessly the fowls upon the trees;
Their feet grow numb and stiff, and loose from
     round
   The limb, they flutter to the earth and freeze,
And lie at morn upon the frozen ground.

But where there are no woods or peaks to stay
  Their force, as on the friendly Texan prairies,
They seem to blow from every point, and play
  About the shivering beasts in wildest mazes,
Like savages around their hapless prey.

The cattle flee toward the south aghast,
  With hair all blown about and bodies drawn.
At sight of man a wishful glance they cast,
  Out of their half-shut eyes; with air forlorn
They hurry on before the cruel blast.

The horses act with almost human skill:
  They tramp the frosty earth with clodded feet,
Until they get behind some wood or hill
  That kindly offers them a free retreat,
Where the winds cannot meet and all is still.

The traveller suffers with his hands and feet
  When caught out where there is no home of man.
He shivers round his fire of light mesquite,
  While teasing fantasies his vision span
Of lighted rooms, and grates of glowing heat.

When the fierce storm that leaves its icy shore,
  And bears dismay and misery o'er the lands,
Chilling all creatures to the inmost core,
  Has spent its force upon the sunny strands,
Then rests the harassed land in peace once more.

The sun throws warm effulgence from above;
  The beasts stand sleeping 'neath his cheerful smiles;
With scarce a breeze the slender twigs to move;
  Kind Nature, to atone for her mad wiles,
With radiant face, caresses us in love.

ROBINSON PEAK.

OLD peak, you are always a friend;
  I stop once more to visit you.
At any time that I may come
  There is spread round a matchless **view.**

I know not when the view is grandest,
  In the bloom of spring, or summer's glow,
When the vales are wrapt in autumnal gloom,
  When the hills are glistening mounds of snow.

The tinted hills surround the plains
  Where runs the sparkling rivulet,
As if upon the rich green sward
  There fell a jeweled carcanet.

With Coleman nestling in the vale—
  Her steeples rise before the eye;
While Santa Anna looms aloft
  Like a sapphire set against the sky.

On the north are isolated peaks
  That make the scenery grotesque;
On the west are alternate chains of hills,
  And gorges grandly picturesque.

The view seems hallowed ground to me,
  For there I roamed when but a boy;
Every vale and peak remembrance brings
  Of keenest sorrow and keenest joy.

SANTA ANNA MOUNTAIN.

LONE mountain ! thy wild grandeur of aspect
    Attracts the emigrant and tourist, too.
    About thee gentle winds are ever stealing;
And the grand view and fresh pure air affect

All life with animation, health, and healing.
Thy summit seems to kiss the concave blue.
Thou art a wonder, lone upon the view—
The handiwork of the great Architect!

We, who are used to thee, as we draw near
  Are startled that such grandeur is so nigh.
Each time before-unnoticed scenes appear;
  The winds steal round thee, and, as they pass by,
Forlornly whistle shrilly in our ear,
  The stealthy autumn winds that live to sigh.

A FACE.

A SWEET face that had charmed my youth,
  Why comes it back from vanished years?
Why, in the stillness of the night,
  Her tender voice falls on my ears
  That with the morning brings hot tears?
  Why make for me a glad surprise
  The waking ne'er can realize?

I saw in dreams a false fair face
  That seemed to pleasingly renew
My life with pure delicious joy.
  My vision was a life to view,
  While all was false—could ne'er come true,
  Even the ties of friendship's bands
  Were sundered by relentless hands.

Her face was mild with wreathed smiles,—
  We roamed the meadow arm in arm,
And talked with playful cheerfulness—
  There was no thought of care to harm
  The golden beauty of the charm;
  The sky shone gladsomely above,
  And all the world smiled on our love.

As with resuscitated life,
　My love comes back once more to me,—
I thought it dead, but only dormant;
　I find again I am not free,
　Bound by the deathless mystery,
　For fear of the harsh world to creep
　Back in the harmless reign of sleep.

A PICTURE.

TAKING a book to while away the time,
　I threw myself beneath the friendly bowers
And read of love, expressed in sweetest rhyme,
　And heedlessly passed by the pleasant hours.

I read, and turned the pages o'er and o'er,
　Came to a pictured face and sculptured arms,
In fair relief, that some resemblance bore
　The royal coronet of earthly charms.

Something was in the picture to excite
　The fond desires of happiness that start,
The longings for the object of delight—
　A panacea for all pains of heart.

I knew where there were rubies never touched,
　And founts of love where one could never sigh;
I knew where there were beauties yet unsearched
　As fine as e'er were seen by mortal eye.

I lost the babble of the limpid brook,
　Where playfully the golden fishes swam;
I lost the rhyming music of my book
　And singing of the birds high on the limb.

I went away in search of my loved one,
　I found her where sublimest music swelled,
While o'er the notes her snowy fingers run;
　There was no joy, no peace, but where she dwelled.

SECURITY.

THICK darkness hovered round the mountain's crest,
    And swiftly played the lightning's fiery streak—
All nature seemed with weariness oppressed,
    And in the somberness I felt most weak.

The restless waves that, with dire aspect, brood
    Upon the bosom of the mighty deep,
Could clasp me with their frightful arms. I would
    Forever in the dismal caverns sleep.

Bright comets shoot across the hemisphere
    And seem to strike within the planets' course,
Might strike together with a clash severe
    And overwhelm me with gigantic force.

I draw back with a dread whene'er I think
    Upon eternal silence and the gloom
Of a releaseless captive, when I sink
    Into the narrow prison of the tomb.

Delightfully secure, though all creation
    As with earthquatic convulsions were riven,
With this globe wrapt in roaming conflagration
    Gleaming with waning light through the clear
        heaven.

The cry and fury of the countless hordes,
    Led by the monarch of the nether realm,
Begirt with breastplates, armed with flaming swords,
    Can do no harm, can ne'er my soul o'erwhelm.

Surprising fact that fills my soul with wonder
    That the meek King of all did die for me.
There is no power can rend our love asunder,
    And I am safe through all eternity.

WESTERN TEXAS.

Written at the close of the drought of 1888.

Two years have farmers plowed and sown their
 fields,
 And watched with anxious eyes all signs of rain,
And hoped that there would be abundant yields ;
 But waiting, toil, and watching were in vain.
No reapers cut and bound the heavy sheaves,
 No buzz of busy threshers filled the air.
The crops were grainless stalks and withered
 leaves,
 And weary hearts were almost in despair.

There seemed to rest o'er all a gloomy spell,
 And people could not talk of other things ;
It was but natural that their minds would dwell
 Despondingly upon the threatenings.
Most of the time the sky was clear and bright,
 Then pallid, filmy vapor with a strain
Of smoke, through which the sun with hazy light
 Shone, as at eve he shines through falling rain.

But in the fall the reeking clouds were lowered
 O'er all the western prairies and the hills ;
For several days the rain in torrents poured
 Overflowing all the rivers and the rills,
Grass sprang from the warm, saturated ground
 The flocks and herds too numerous to name,
That grazed in vale, on hillside, and the mound,
 Were rolling fat before the winter came.

Two years without a harvest, England would
 Have been a miserable and helpless isle,
And China would have been a solitude.
 I muse upon it with a joyous smile.
We have passed through the gloomy time together,
 And only good comes of the evil dearth :
We have a warmer love for one another,
 And feel more grateful to the bounteous earth.

I sit here by my window, breathing sweet
  Aroma wafted o'er the balmy plain ;
I see the rustling, swaying corn, the wheat
  And oats just ripening into golden grain ;
Beyond are crystal streams where cattle drink.
  There is new life in every blade and shoot,
Luxuriant branches of the fruit-trees sink
  Down, overburdened with clustered fruit.

Delightful country, richest, best to me ;
  For thou hast been my youthful happy home.
I like in thy pure atmosphere to be,
  And o'er thy lovely hills and plains to roam.
Now as the phœnix from its ashes rose,
  Thou risest with more than whilom loveliness,
Where was but dust now an abundance grows
  And Cornucopia scatters to excess.

THE OLD STORY.

THE trees were sparsely tinged with green,
  First smile of Spring shone everywhere.
In a room of pale gold, dreamy sheen,
  Stood two, a man and lady fair.
Red drapery muffled the glaring light
  That threw o'er all an aspect dull,
And, falling upon her tresses bright,
  Made her surpassingly beautiful.

Caressing ringlets fell to deck
  Her rosy cheeks and temples fair,
The chain that clasped her lily-white neck
  Seemed jealous of its fortune there.
As the first martyr gazed upon
  The beauties of the heavenly throne,
The eyes without comparison
  He saw as they shone in his own.

Sublimely noble was her face.
  The eyes sparkled with latent ire;
A few faint flushes he could trace
  That gleamed with a subdued fire.
But still he lingered there to feast
  His eyes upon that longed-for face;
In anger dearer far increased
  Than lived in any other place.

He would from off his life have given years
  To have pressed a kiss upon her lips,
Yet she would not, with pouting fears,
  Suffer him to touch her finger tips.
The scene was a trifle, transitory,
  Yet such as often seen by men;
It was only the old, old story,
  He loved, but was not loved again.

WEST TEXAS SHEPHERD.

HE lets his flocks feed slowly forth at morn,
  As the first sunbeams strike the distant view;
The fresh-blown flowers hills and vales adorn,
  The lilies sparkle with the crystal dew,
Like snowy hands with pearls of the Orient.
  He turns them homeward when far down the sphere
Of his diurnal course the sun is bent,
  Then waits the lengthening shadow creeping near,
Until he sinks into the Occident.

The hours drag slowly in midsummer days:
  At morn and eve the lambs play on the banks,
The ewes bleat to them, and around them graze.
  They cease to feed, the lambs their buoyant pranks,
When the vales quiver in the sultry heat.
  They gather in small bunches as they run,
With heads down, panting, and with smothered bleat,
  To huddle in the shade until the sun
Is low before they leave the cool retreat,

He loves his slicker as his truest friend,
　When cumuli like snow-capped peaks arise,
And lurid flames the frightful mountains rend,
　Through which peep far-off tranquil summer skies.
On the bare prairies the unchecked wind fleets,
　So swiftly that it takes his breath away,
And, roaring, lifts the driven icy sheets,
　And drenches and redrenches him with spray,
While on his unsheltered head the hail-storm beats.

The days grow short and autumn hues appear;
　The clouds brood o'er the earth like sable wings;
The drizzle, mist, and sleet fall cold and drear
　As winter comes, and all its fury brings.
The winds sweep by, and shriek like forlorn fiends;
　The sheep are restless, roving here and there,
And only stop to feed in deep ravines,
　Safe from the raging of the upper air.
From the fell blast some cliff the shepherd screens.

Exposed alike to nature's calm or strife,
　He feels himself a portion of the wild,
Men pass him by, and useless seems his life.
　Oh, how it glads him if a careless child
Will call and cheer his spirit as it wanes.
　He pets his dog as if some human thing,
And comes to like the lone trees of the plains;
　He finds companions in the cliff and spring,
And wonders why his dog with him remains.

LONGINGS.

I.

My Bonnibel, I can not tell
　Thee what thou art to me,
In words that link all that I think
　In tranquil hours of thee.
A vision bright in a world of night,
　In thee I ever see.

II.

When the evening breeze steals through the trees
    With the perfume of roses,
'Neath flowered vine, where roses twine
    In variegated posies,
My soul doth long for thine in song,
    And all its warmth discloses.

III.

Would I could touch—is it too much?
    Thy snowy hands once more ;
Thy ruby lips that quite eclipse
    The Inca's golden store,
A blushing wreath round pearly teeth,
    That none have touched before.

IV.

The antelope feeds on the slope,
    I think of thee again ;
Its trim head raises, wildly gazes
    About o'er all the plain,
Flees wild with fear as I come near,
    Though no fear need entertain.

V.

There is a land of golden sand
    And ever-foliaged trees,
Where gorgeous tints of the sun's prints
    Afford a weird heart-ease,
We would forget there more to fret
    At things that do displease.

VI.

I cannot bear strange eyes to stare
    Upon thy precious form,
Lest that, perchance, their careless glance
    Thy purity would harm—
Without longings and jealous stings,
    And passion's latent storm.

VII.

It often seems to me in dreams
    That thou art lost to me,
Thy heart benign, thine eyes divine,
    Another holds in fee,—
My hope then sinks adown the brinks,
    Into a troubled sea.

VIII.

Life is flying, hope is dying,
    And still thou art not near.
In every place thy glowing face
    Would dispel every fear.
My whole life's length, all passion's strength,
    Is for thy love, my dear.

M. T. YATES

THE light shot o'er a darkened hemisphere,
And he was one ray of that glorious light.
Long centuries of superstitious night
Had brooded o'er a mighty continent,
And thicker grew, defying light and truth,
Until the darkness seemed impenetrable.

He turned his back upon his native land,
His home, and the companions of his youth ;
And crossed the ocean, landing on the shore
Of a strange country that he did not know,
With his loving companion at his side.
Encouraged by the Spirit from on high,
And mind illumined with the meeting rays
That the great suns of human knowledge threw
Upon his way—the wisdom of his time,
And all refinements of the classic Greek,
And master of the secret powers of song,
He went among a people, strange in face
And garb, and in peculiar customs taught.
Against the errors of the centuries
He taught them of the Cross of Calvary.

His country was rent by intestine war,
And Christian fought with Christian, brother with
    brother.
His native land was drenched with the blood
Of her own sons, and wept over their deeds ;
But his warfare was peace, the rest in Christ.
He mixed not in the carnage of his home,
And turned not from his work to look on them.
And a strange war was raging round his post,
For he was in the midst of heathen rage
And all the awful weirdness of their war,
But he was calm. Peace, Peace ! was his watchword.
He led the conquest of the Prince of Peace,
He waved His banner and ne'er let it drop,
Amid war, rage, and superstitious strife
Of the degenerate children of the earth.

His good was not only in heathen lands ;
The influence of his pure, noble life
Was not closed in by deserts or by seas,
Or distance, continents, or mountains, isles,
But it extended to remotest land,
And took the hearts of those whom he knew not.
For on the western plains my mother took
Me on her knee and told me of a friend
Of her youth, in her North Carolina home,
At dear Wake Forest ; and that she knew him
When she was young made it dearer to me.
She spoke of the long years that he had toiled
A missionary in far-off Shanghai ;
And I longed to do noble things myself.

Forty-two years he remained at his post,
And spoke of decades as but days of work,
As he toiled to redeem a world from sin—
A hero in the service of his God,
The prince of His embassadors ! to bear
Glad tidings to the souls perishing in night.
Forty-two years—nearly twice my own age—
Yet I have known despair, what suffering is,

Discouragement, and fainting by the way,
With nothing grand or noble in my lot.
The greatest missionary of the world,
Grander than poet, soldier, statesman, king,
One of North Carolina's noblest sons,—
An unknown Texan lays a fading wreath
Of his obscure muse on thy foreign grave.

IZORA.

When a small boy at school an attachment I formed
For a lovely young lady, whose age quite disarmed
That timidity of bashful lovers when young,
And the strongest of friendships in sweetness up-
    sprung.

I loved her with unadulterated platonic love,
It was too good for earth, it belonged but above.
You will not censure me, I am sure, you all know
How very little boys love grown young ladies so.

Not a word about love was between us e'er spoken,
Nor any of lovers' smiles, blushes, or affectionate
    token,
But in the bright hours of youth's blissful portions
We lived in true friendship with all its devotions.
She was so kind, sweet, patient, I always knew where
Was one lovely being who would my studies gladly
    share.

She is married now, and has children of her own,
But still I often think of our friendship when alone.
What a beautiful halo it throws round my youth!
No cross words or hard feelings or actions unruth.
Look back as I will, there is nothing to regret,
No rudeness or resentment we all like to forget;
But all was so sweet, perfect, peaceful, and good,
That it cheers me to think o'er it in solitude.

Many laughed at our friendship and said it was
    naught;
But since all things have proved that they spoke
    without thought.
Having since endured scorn, deceit, rebuffs without
    end,
I have now learned to know the true worth of a
    friend;
And that which all laughed at as youth's wild oats
    sown,
Was the wisest and noblest thing of life I have known.

Her face, oh! how radiant with animated sweetness,
Where thought portrayed thought in marvelous fleet-
    ness.
I gazed on its beauty, but I prized it not then
As now I would, could those joyous times come again.
I have looked at the sun in his dazzling noontide
Unconscious of his splendor till my eyes turned aside,
And his image floated 'tween them and all that was
    near :   [appear.
Turn and look where I would, the bright spots would
Then I thought of the great luminary of light
That shone with such power that it still dazed my
    sight.
Her voice, when she spoke to me in softness of feel-
    ing
Was as the tones of lovers their emotions revealing,
When their voices in harmonious cadence are set
To the sad, melting music of a love-lorn duet.
I have listened to the variations of " Home, sweet
    Home,"
And long afterwards would the refrains tender come
And sound in my ears, and while at work would me
    haunt,
Rising, falling, throughout the changes as its wont.
So her voice often rings in its soft changing moods
In my memory when alone in life's solitudes,
Now it rings with gladness, now it melts to low
    moans,

Now softly it trembles in lovers' rapturous tones—
So natural, so sweet, so striking, so much like her
I look up to behold her, it seems she is near.

In childhood I have often seen children pluck flowers
While at play in the recesses of cool shady bowers,
And put them 'neath a glass in a hole in the ground,
And left on the glass a place with the cold earth
  around.
The next morning they peeped through the glass
  down on them,
And they glowed with a brighter hue than when on
  the stem.
The dark night had brightened them with the spark-
  ling dew,
And the sunlight fell on them, enhancing the view.

Now, back through the shadow that has settled o'er
  me,
These detached flowers of memory through a glass I
  still see ;
The darkness closes round them, but the light still
  remains,
And, despite disappointments, grief, sorrow and pains,
These flowerets become brighter and fresher with
  time.
And now as I look on them seem divine, seem sub-
  lime.
Tears falling upon them only brighten their hue,
And the drops wash the glass, transparing the view.

A REVERIE.

Once I was canopied by bowers green,
      And all around was glad ; the flowers
          Partook the skyey tinges.
I mused upon the beauties I had seen
      Or created in idle hours,
          Of perfectness of things.

A little girl, with voice so sweet and kind,
    Pressed her plump lips and cheeks against
        The thin lips and wan cheeks
Of an aged woman, wrinkled, meek and blind.
    Her golden tresses were enhanced
        By threads in silver streaks.

A great, big boy who loves his mother so,
    Looked lovingly upon her face.
        To her sweet words he said ;
He thought her young and beautiful, alhtough
    Long years of care had left their trace,
        And the bloom of youth had fled.

Two beings wed in first love's blissful waking,
    Ere either had known love beside,
        Their love, true love requiting.
For no one either loved—no hearts were breaking
    With hopeless love for groom or bride,
        When marriage is a blighting.

A perfect woman with angelic mien,
    The loveliest creature here below,
        For whom all songs are sung,
Made a fresh wreath of laurels ever green
    And placed it round the poet's brow,
        While his heart with grief was wrung.

DEAD MAN'S CROSSING.

SHE was a young lady teacher from the old states who had come to Texas to seek employment, and alighted from the cars at a small western town. Some friends of hers had moved west some years before and settled in this town. She was drawn to this town because she felt so lonesome in a strange land— a situation in which we all are glad to be near some old friends. Her friends did all they could to secure her a place to teach in the schools, but to no avail.

But one day a rich ranchman from the west came to town in quest of a governess who had grit enough to face the hardships of camp life and undertake the management of his children. He heard of Marion Urser, and came to see her, and offered her better wages than she had ever received before. On making inquiries she found that this ranchman was well known to many people in the town, and all spoke well of him and his family, and said that she could not find a better place ; but at the same time dissuaded her from going on account of the lonely isolated life she must lead, so different from what she had been used to. But she consented to go, and when the time came to start even the rough ranchman, when he noticed her slender form, lovely face, and small white hands, said good-naturedly :

"I don't want yer ter go unless yer wantter, Miss, fur it's mighty lonesome out thar,—not like what you're use ter. We are all rough out thar, and yer'l see none but dirty men. Wife and me were once used ter polite 'siety, but we've got as bad as any of 'um."

"Oh! do not make me a coward," she said, smiling sweetly. "I ought to be able to stand what your wife and the rest of the women do."

"Unless yer think yer can manage the young uns, yer'd better not go , fer they're as wild as the young cyotes that howl round 'um," he remonstrated.

But Marion Urser looked up into the honest eyes of the plain man and felt that she need fear nothing while under his care.

On the way to the ranch the old man did not know what to talk about that would interest the accomplished young lady, but once he said, smiling blandly : "We've ugly names fur places out in our country, and I thought I'd better not tell yer the name uv our ranch, fearing it 'ud prejudice you agin it afore yer got thar."

"O, tell me, I will not get prejudiced, I am sure I will not," she said interestedly.

"Dead Man's Crossing on Devil's River."

Marion made no reply, but admitted to herself that it was a rather hard name.

Late one evening they reached Mr. Stedman's ranch. The sheep were being driven home for the night, and the lambs filled the air with their cries, and many cattle were grazing on the rounded hills. As they drove up, Marion looked about her, there were several tents and shanties in view. Here was where she was to make her home.

She was lonesome for a few days. The rough life was revolting to her refined nature, but she gradually got to liking it. She immediately made friends of the children—they came to idolize her. Although wild, they were good-hearted, and she learned to love them as well as they did her. There were many men about the ranch whom she saw often, and all were so kind to her and seemed so glad that she had come to live among them. But everything was so wild and strange. All day she heard the bleating of the sheep and the lowing of the cattle. At night she heard the lonesome howling of the wolves, and far down in the gorges of the river the screaming of the cougar, which she thought unmistakably the cry of a woman in distress.

One time she asked Mrs. Stedman how the ranch received such a frightful name. The good woman told her a long story, how the crossing on Devil's River near their ranch was the only one either way, up or down the river, for many miles ; for the river ran through the plains and hills and mounds, and one could see no signs of a river until he stood upon the brink of a chasm and heard the fretting of the water as it ran over the rocks in the depths below. The river ran through this chasm for many miles before there was any break in the jagged walls down in the earth where a crossing could be effected. One day some cowboys were chasing a wild cat with dogs, when it ran into a bunch of bushes near this crossing, and when the boys went into the clump, they found a little glade upon which lay scattered about the

bones and the tattered, almost rotten, clothes of a
man.   In a detached pocket they found a purse
containing some gold and silver and a roll of rotten
bills.   A diamond ring still encircled the bone of one
of his little fingers.   He was a man of some years;
for he had lost several teeth and some that remained
were plugged, and the shining metal glittered in the
grinning skull that was turned upward toward the
sun.   He could not have been killed for his money,
as many had been in these wilds.   It was supposed
that he was travelling through the country during the
drouth of a few years before, and had travelled long
through the heat before finding the crossing, and had
taken a fever and crawled into the bushes to obtain
shelter from the sun, and there died all alone.   Ever
since the crossing had gone by the name of "Dead
Man's Crossing."

One evening while Marion was strolling about
with the children, they came to a path that led over
the brink into the river, and she heard the murmur
of the stream beneath.

" Why does this path run right over the brink ? "
she asked.

" This is the path to the spring," both children
answered at once, with a look of surprise depicted
upon their faces.   " Come and look over," they went
on, taking her by the hands.   She allowed herself to
be led, but eased up carefully and peered over the
brink.   Her head became dizzy, for the stream was
running swiftly over the rocks far down in the earth.
A ladder made of ropes was suspended from the
bank down to a spring that gurgled up from the
gravel surrounded by rocks safe from the stream.
The sun shone down the gorge, and the clear stream
trickling down do the river sparkled like a string of
jewels.

She did not remain lonesome long.   Something
strange and wild happened nearly every day to
interest her.   One morning at the breakfast-table
Mr. Stedman related that a cougar had broken into

one of the sheep pens the night before and killed a lamb before one of the herders shot and killed him. Immediately after breakfast, Marion and the children retired to the vacated sheep pen to see the prize. They gazed long upon the yellow striped monster stretched out before them. But turned away in sadness when they saw the innocent victim lying near by with only a crimson spot on its throat.

One summer day when the sun shone mildly upon the purple hills where the sheep were huddled under the trees, and the cattle had come down to the crossing to drink, and the children had gone to play in the shady groves, Marion Urser strolled down the river, lost in reverie of the past. She did not remember herself until she came suddenly upon a horse, richly caparisoned, standing in the shade of a tree. She was near the crossing. A man was lying under the tree near the horse. They saw each other simultaneously, and she took him to be a Mexican, and, feeling extremely uneasy, started to retreat. But the man motioned his hand for her to come nearer. She stood for some moments looking at him. She knew from his look that he must be in distress. Mrs. Stedman's story of the man who died all alone near the same place came to her mind, with all the force of its sadness about it. She could not go away and leave him. She drew nearer, and discovered that he was not a Mexican but a handsome, nicely-dressed young man, his face haggard with sickness.

" My good angel, where did you come from ?" he said, smiling faintly and trying to rise from the ground, but sank back utterly exhausted.

" I live a short distance up the river. Are you sick ? Can I do anything for you ?" she asked anxiously.

He did not answer her immediately but lay watching her. " Where could you have come from to rise up so suddenly upon these desolate wilds ? You are the loveliest being I ever saw."

Marion blushed, but answered only with an inquiring look of her eyes.

"I am sick. I think I am crazy with a fever. I have ridden hard, for I have been pursued by two Mexicans who have been trying to murder and rob me. They are after me now. But you can do nothing for me, my good angel, unless you can tell me where I can find protection and repose."

His face was flushed from the exertion, which made his already handsome features wonderfully beautiful; and she had not heard any one speak with such perfect accent since she had been in the western country.

"I shall be gone but a few minutes. I will get Mr. Stedman to come down and get you;" and before he could think she was gone.

Marion hurried back to the house and told Mr. Stedman all about the sick man whom she had found; how he was pursued by Mexicans seeking his life. No time was lost. The hack and team were made ready, and Mr. Stedman drove swiftly to the place where the sick man lay, Marion being guide. The horse was grazing leisurely about his sick master, but just as Mr. Stedman and Marion alighted from the hack he gave a loud snort and looked wildly toward the river. Marion cast a startled glance at Mr. Stedman. Two Mexicans came galloping toward them from the river. But as soon as they saw a man and woman, wheeled their horses and rode around.

"Did you ever shoot a revolver, Miss Marion?" Mr. Stedman asked.

"Yes, sir!" she replied quickly. "We used to practice often at home."

"Will you take one of these and use it if those Mexicans return and offer fight?"

"Yes, sir," she replied firmly, taking the proffered weapon.

They then went to where the wayfarer lay. He was unconscious of the danger that had just threatened him and the beautiful girl standing over him who had been the means of saving his life ; for he was sleeping soundly. They took him up gently and placed him in the hack. He roused but did not wake. They drove slowly to the house ; and a cowboy was dispatched for the nearest doctor. All night the sick man lay in a stupor as the kind people of the ranch nursed him. But the next morning he seemed awake to all around. He saw Marion standing near his bed, and said, attempting to smile :

"You are the angel that appeared to me on the river. Am I safe now?"

"Yes, you are safe," she said, gently. "But you need rest ; compose yourself and sleep."

Later on the doctor came, but said it was a bad case of typhoid fever, and he could hardly be hoped to get well.

Many days the stranger lay near death. None knew his name. There might have been papers about his clothing which could have given some clue as to who he was or the place of his destination, but no one examined them. By and by the crisis passed, and he began to improve. Marion was with him much of the time, and talked so pleasantly that he was scarcely conscious of the loneliness of convalescence.

"All seems so strange," he said to her one day. "My sickness has seemed like a pleasant dream, for you have been so good to me. I have no idea how long I have been here." This was spoken in the manner of a question, and, although Marion blushed at the compliment, she answered, "You have been here four weeks."

"Oh! I must be up and about," he said, uneasily.

"The doctor said you must stay about the house a week longer," she reminded sweetly, and he said nothing more.

Marion Urser went to take a walk that evening as usual, but her mind was full of guesses about their strange visitor. She tried to think of something else, but the handsome unknown would return to her thoughts again. "Why should I think of him?" she

asked herself. " He may be married, he is old enough.
Well, I am getting on in years. There ! I am thinking of him again."

A week passed. The visitor talked much of leaving; and Marion had a presentiment that he would
say something to her before he left, and she was not
surprised, although she pretended to be, when he said
to her: " I would like to talk to you alone before I go.
Will you walk with me down the river ? "

" Yes," was all she replied, and they walked slowly
along the bank of the river.

" I have been very strange to you, Miss Urser, I
know. I have never told you my name," and he
glanced at her and saw that inquiring look of the eyes
that he saw that day under the tree. " My name is
George Beyon. You may think me married, but I am
not, although I am old enough to be. I cannot tell
you where I live, for I travel about so much. Sometimes I am in southern Texas, then in Mexico." By
this time they had reached the tree under which
Marion had found George Beyon that day, but she did
not notice it until he said softly: " Let us sit down
under this tree, for I love it because it was where I
first saw you." These remarks made Marion glad,
but she turned her face away and sat down.

" Miss Marion, there is no use in saying any unnec-
essary words," he went on. "I love you, and have
brought you down to this tree to ask you to be my
wife." This was making love and coming to the
point in a purely Texas fashion, yet Marion Urser
thought that there was an ineffable charm about it.

She was still silent, and he took her white, delicate
hands into his, and she did not try to draw them
away. This gave him hope. " Will you take me
just as I am, Miss Marion ? " he pleaded. " you know
nothing about me, but if it be in human power I will
make you happy."

" Yes, I will be your wife whatever may come; I
have come to love you so well," she replied earnestly.

" Oh! what have I found and won here where I expected nothing! You have made me happier than I have ever hoped to be. I had no hope of winning you."

The subject was dropped there, and they returned to the ranch, walking slowly, and plucking the wildflowers that grew beside the path, and chatting merrily.

They separated at the steps, and Marion proceeded to her room, there to think over the thing that had happened. Somehow there was a strangeness about the affair that frightened her. Everything had taken place so quickly. Yet she could find nothing to regret. She saw nothing more that day of Mr. Beyon except a glimpse of him from her window as he was riding off with Mr. Stedman that evening. But the next morning he came to her.

"Marion, my love—for I know I can call you that now—" he began, taking her hands in his, and looking lovingly into her eyes, "I must go away this morning, and will be gone about a month. Do you think that you will not change your mind by that time, but will be ready to marry me when I return?"

"O yes, my dear George, I will marry you any time. I know I cannot change. How lonesome I shall be while you are gone. But I shall think of you all the time, and watch anxiously for your return."

"You will give me a kiss, my darling, will you not?" he said, and he looked so handsome, true and noble, that she unhesitatingly kissed him, and he returned it and was gone. Marion stood watching him as he rode away, her eyes suffused with tears. She loved this man better than she had ever supposed that she could love any one on so short an acquaintance.

The Stedmans became even more kind to her than before Mr. Beyon took his departure. A new governess was procured, and she lived in perfect ease. The family would not let her teach the children, in spite of her protestations. The world seemed sud-

denly transformed into a paradise to her, and she
was satisfied that Mr. Beyon had told the Stedmans
of their engagement.   She was lonesome sometimes,
but not for long; for her passionate lover could not
stay away, but returned unexpectedly and brought
everything for the marriage, and Marion Urser stood
beside the man she had found and rescued upon the
lonely river, and was joined to him for life.

But I have not told all.   There are two lives the
remainders of which are not lived, that I could not
describe if I wished.   Lives of perfect love and happiness, that defy the power of my pen.   Marion Urser
found the opening joy of her life in a land which she
had dreaded to come to dwell in, a lonely home in a
wild and strange country.   Her husband took her
away to his home in a sunny clime, where they live
surrounded by all the comfort and happiness which
wealth and love can make in a lovely home in a
land of perennial flowers.

AN INNOCENT DECEPTION.

"Oh! how lonesome it is here," cried handsome
William Smitts, impatiently twirling his long, black,
romantic moustache between his fingers.   "I have
fished until there are no more fish in the creek.   I
have hunted until there is nothing more to shoot;
and there is not a pretty girl in all the land.   I shall
surely die of *ennui* if I stay here any longer."

"Why, Will, you naughty boy," cried his sister-in-
law, with feigned provokiveness, as she came to the
door and looked out at him where he sat on the
piazza.   "I have a message for Mrs. Silven, and I
want to send it by you, for I think you sorely need
the exercise.   I know you will like them; they are
such nice people.   I hope to get better acquainted
with them in the future."

"All right!" he exclaimed, jumping from the chair.
So, in a few minutes, he was riding along the road,

whistling absent-mindedly. He was just from college, and had come to take a rest with his brother, who had just moved out to his western home. They had not become very well acquainted with their neighbors, and John Smitts, not liking to leave his family alone, had taken the time while William was with them to go away and attend to some business which he had been long delaying, and William was left to take care of the place.

He reached the gate, and found himself in front of a fine mansion, with beautiful shrubbery growing on either side of the walk which ran from the gate to the house. He had seen the house from the distance before while out hunting, but had seen nothing of its magnificence.

He knocked, and a pleasant lady's voice said, " come in." He opened the door, and within the room was neat to perfection, and there stood before him a beautiful young woman, and beside her three or four blooming children. " Mrs. Silven, I suppose? Mr. Smitts," he said in his most polite air. The lady merely bowed. He delivered the message, and in a short time took his departure.

All the way home he was haunted by a fresh young face, and wondered how Mrs. Silven could look so young and fair.

That day at dinner, as soon as he had sat down, he said, " What a very handsome woman Mrs. Silven is. Did you ever notice it ? "

" Oh, yes ! she is the most lovely lady I have seen in this country," replied Mrs. Smitts, carelessly, not paying any attention to his remarks about Mrs. Silven's good looks any more than any man would say in praise of another man's wife.

After that visit, William would never go about the Silven's residence again. Try as she would, Mrs. Smitts could in no way persuade him to go there any more.

" Why do you always refuse to go to Mr. Silven's, Will ? You always go everywhere else I want you to.

It looks like you would be glad to go, they are such nice people," she said to him one morning after he had made some excuse or another when she wanted him to go to Mr. Silven's.

"I do not know," he replied, carelessly. "I have an aversion to it somehow."

He told the truth when he said he did not know the reason why he did not like to go to Mr. Silven's—at least he could not have put that reason into words. But he did not have an aversion to the place. While out hunting, he would go near the house, and gaze long and wistfully at it, as if there was some great attraction for him there. Still he could not understand why he did so.

A week later William took Mrs. Smitts and the children to a picnic, and leaving her to talk to the ladies, he wandered over the grounds with the children. As he was walking about talking lightly to them, perchance, he came across Mrs. Silven and her children. He bowed politely and she blushed modestly when she recognized him. William went away wondering what it was about Mrs. Silven which was so captivating.

That evening as they drove home, Mrs. Smitts tried in vain to rally him into a conversation. He was thinking of the woman who had gained such ascendency over him under such unpropitious circumstances. Why did she blush crimson, and her eyes droop with girlish modesty whenever she saw him?

A week later William rode by the Silven mansion, and beheld the woman who had bewitched him, sitting upon the portico. She made a beautiful picture, embowered among the vines, her hair flowing loose, and the auburn tresses played about the plump, white neck. A beautiful vision flashed athwart his mind. What if some day he should have such a residence as that, and such a lady for his bride! He rode on—he could not bear to gaze. He was dazzled by so much loveliness.

All the way home he upbraided himself for his

weakness. " Will Smitts, you are a fool," he would
say to himself. " After having so many girls at college lavish their affections upon you, and none could
outstrip you in learning, now to fall hopelessly in
love with a married woman!" And he shivered as
he thought of it.

If William Smitts had lost confidence in his
strength of mind, he was not the only one. Beautiful Lizzie Silven had seen him as he passed by that
day, and immediately retired to her magnificent bou-
doir, her tender heart fluttering strangely. She
blushed the first time she saw this man, and he seemed
to have a strange influence over her. This influence
had increased every day, and now had completely
overpowered her. She was the incarnation of Reverie. She did not speak, but meditated upon things
she had never thought of before. How sweet it
would be to have such a man for a lover, and she
imagined him coming with his handsome face wear-
ing its sweetest expression, and his voice its softest
resonance thrilling her soul, making love to her.
Her fancy world was too lovely, and she bethought
herself. Ah! he was a married man.

One day William came blustering into the house,
not knowing that any one was present, when he saw
a noble-looking, middle-aged lady, and something
looked familiar about her as he took her in at a
glance.

" Why, Will! you silly boy," cried Mrs. Smitts, a
ring of mischief in her voice, " let me introduce you
to Mrs. Silven. Mrs. Silven says," she went on without stopping, " that she has been away all the time;
and that Lizzie had just come back from school, and
she left her to take care of the children while she was
gone; and you have been taking her for her mother
all the time. You foolish boy, how will you ever
make apologies to Miss Lizzie? Oh! I know it will
all be right when I tell her how often I listened to
the praises of Mrs. Silven, and I know the real Mrs.
Silven will not care."

"There are two sides to the affair," said Mrs. Silven, laughing, and looking archly at William. "Lizzie has taken you to be Mr. John Smitts, and has been talking to me a great deal about him."

William made his escape as soon as possible, and went to walk in the garden. He could hardly stay upon the earth. Heaven itself is but a little more blissful than his soul was at that moment. There was just a little leaven of trouble in his universe of joy—just enough to make him realize that he was upon the earth. It was that which always troubles the heart of man after the first joy of true love is awakened in his breast. What if she had a lover, and he already possessed her heart? He could not bear to think of it. He would not be in suspense, he could not stand to be. He would go to her and tell her of his great love for her and have his life made happy or blasted by her innocent lips; and then he thought of where he was, and of the stern reality of .things. He must wait.

He spent the night in flitting dreams of horror; he was in that state of mind in which we cannot rest. Every time he closed his eyes, he could see another leading his beloved to the altar. She looked so lovely in the foamy attire of a bride, and so innocent, and transcendently beautiful beside a man who was an entire stranger to him; she was looking up so sweetly into his face, and seemed so happy to be near him. And then he would imagine some one crying in his ears: "Too late, too late!" Such dreams drove him to distraction. When he awoke, he could hardly think it possible that they had not really happened—that he had not even made an effort to win her. She was young, and probably had never known of love, and he might yet gain the affections of the lovely creature whom he had learned to love so well in the last few weeks of his life.

The next morning was faultlessly beautiful. The sun was just warm enough to be pleasant, and beasts and birds alike enjoyed the perfect day. William

Smitts, in harmony with all about him, felt a keen sense of joy as he wandered aimlessly through the fields and down by the creek where he was wont to fish. But the placid water, whose surface was only broken now and then by the flounder of a trout, had no attractions for him now.

He still kept walking, and did not have sense enough to see that he was getting on the Silven lands, when he came suddenly upon the creatress of his troubles. She was carelessly dressed in white, which looked pleasant in the warm summer day, and made her look as fresh and beautiful as a rose in the morning. She held a fishing-pole in her delicate hands, and was watching the cork, for a fish was nibbling just then, so she did not see him. The natural impression which first took possession of him suggested that he flee at once—he had no business there. But love suggested nothing of the kind; and William Smitts was a Texas youth and cared not for expenses, but marched forth to untried fields undaunted.

He came nearer; and she looked up and saw him. Her face became the home of blushes, and he said in his sweetest voice, " Miss Silven, I will introduce myself again, although we are so well acquainted. I did not know until yesterday who you were, and you did not know who I was. I am William Smitts, brother to John Smitts who lives at the next house."

" Yes," she said smiling, while all embarrassment vanished, I thought you were Mr. John Smitts, and what a laughable delusion! I am ashamed of it. Mother told me all about it when she came home last night."

" I do not think it ridiculous," he replied thoughtfully. " It has been the most interesting event of my life."

She glanced up at him quickly, and the rose-tints came to her cheeks; and, as he began to speak, the most fortunate thing happened. She had let the pole drop while talking, and now something had seized the hook and was carrying line, pole, and all away.

William grabbed the pole mechanically just before it was out of reach, and drew the fluttering, marble-lined trout upon the bank, where he lay shining like silver.

" Oh, how beautiful he is ! " she cried, clapping her hands with delight. " You bring luck, Mr. Smitts."

The fish seemed to put them at the most intimate ease.

" I have something I am dying to tell you, Miss Silven," he continued, with renewed hopes. " But I am afraid you will be angry with me."

" Oh ! I would not get angry at anything," she replied lightly. "I am in an excellently good humor to-day."

" I have learned to love you, Miss Lizzie," he said earnestly and slowly, as if he was studying the effect of his words upon his companion, " as never man loved woman before, while I yet thought you were the wife of another ; and now I love you still more because there is hope."

Here was the handsome lover she had wished for, making love to her in the most passionate manner ; and she was young and enthusiastic, and knew not what she said ; for love did it all.

" I am so glad. What a great burden is removed from my heart." Here she seemed to remember herself and turned her face from him.

" O, Miss Lizzie," he cried eagerly, "tell me if you think you can ever care for me. If not, I will go away and try to forget."

" Oh ! do not go away," she said, a troubled expression upon her face. "I think I have always loved you, in my dreams of the ideal ; and when I saw you and thought you were somebody else, I was silly enough to love you beyond my power to express." Her cheeks were crimson and her eyes were brilliant with love.

He did not kiss her as they do in novels ; her lips were too sacred to him. But he took her hands in his, and looking into her face as in the face of an angel, said :

" My Lizzie, I know we will be happy. For we were intended for each other. An unseen power knit our souls together with an undying love when we thought we must be forever separated from each other, for the broadest gulf that can separate the love of a man and woman, rolled, in our imaginations, between us."

And innocent Lizzie Silven acquiesced in everything he said ; and looked angelically beautiful at that moment as she nestled close to him. And William Smitts's vision of a magnificent mansion and a lovely bride was realized.

A RANGER'S FORTUNE.

I.

" THEY do not know that we are in pursuit, or intend to stand a fight in those hills," said the captain of a company of Texas Rangers, pointing to a range of purple-tinted hills slowly rising in the distance.

They had found the trail that morning, and from the signs, they knew that the Indians could be but a few hours in advance. At this remark of the captain, they doubled their speed, and rode on in silence. Each one seemed to be in too deep a study to think of talking.

It was a lovely day in June, and every now and then a lark soared aloft, singing merrily ; and the grasshoppers kept up a continued buzz, flying up before the horses. They looked behind them and beheld the boundless, rolling prairies ; and before them the hills rose higher and higher, and more apparent because of their rugged outlines.

While hurrying across a dog-town, one of the men happened to look down, and immediately exclaimed, " I see something like a wagon track ! " As this was spoken, the company halted, and the captain dismounted, and, after looking carefully about him, said, with a look of surprise, "It is a hack track! They do not know that they are pursued, or they would not try to take along all of their booty. They may not be Indians; but I cannot understand, if they are travelers or hunters, why they are evidently traveling so fast. For they certainly could not have passed along here more than two hours ago, and yet they are out of sight, although I can see with my glasses many miles away."

Then all relapsed into silence; they were awed at the prospects of a fight with the savages. No sound was heard, but the prairie dog's shrill bark, and the regular tramping of the horse's feet upon the sod. The cool and gentle breezes, those silent wanderers of the plains, just pressed their lips upon their foreheads and passed on, leaving them wonderfully refreshed.

At last they turned into a canyon and made their way through tangled chaparral and thorny cactus. The leader halted suddenly, and exclaimed in an excited tone, "A smoke!" and pointed up an opening in the hills. Yes, there was the blue and curling smoke, which mounted upward to the summer sky. The captain said, "Halt!" in an undertone. He then dismounted and crawled behind the undergrowth to the top of a point, and putting his glasses to his eyes, turned them in the direction of the smoke. He saw a vehicle, and one or two Indians moving about and something that looked like several lying in the shade. Beyond the camp were about fifty horses, feeding peacefully in a cove made by a turn in the hills. When he came down to his companions, he said, "They do not know that we are on their trail. They came into this canyon only that they might not be discovered by the smoke while waiting for their horses to graze. We cannot get a better time to attack them than now."

At this they moved stealthily forward until they came to the last clump of bushes that hid them from the Indians. The captain cried, "Charge!" in a firm tone.

The Indians heard the tramp of the horses' feet upon the gravel, and were in commotion in a moment. They sprang for their arms, but before they could reach them the rangers were upon them.

The rangers checked their horses and fired, and the sound echoed and re-echoed through the hills; and every shot was to good effect.

Was it a ghost? a fairy? an angel? They did not know.

For just then two powerful savages led out a beautiful girl and placed her between them and the rangers. She was dressed in mourning; her hair hung loose, and the gentle breezes that stole their way through the opening in the hills made it undulate about her pallid face, and lie in ripples upon her snowy neck. They gazed for a moment spell-bound at the wonderful spectacle, then turned of one accord and rushed back to the covert of the hill, and stood and looked at one another for some time before any one spoke.

"We shall have to take her from them immediately, or they will make their escape. For they do not intend that we shall fight them while they have her," said Bob Randon, a young man of six and twenty, with earnest blue eyes, and handsome sunburnt, and almost feminine features.

"Yes," said the captain, "if we try to fight them, they will place her where a ball will be sure to strike her, or they will scalp her before our eyes."

This seemed to put a new determination into Bob. His face was flushed as he exclaimed, "I tell you what I will do! If you all will charge upon them with me I will rush in among them and carry her off or lose my life in the attempt."

"It will be a dangerous undertaking, Bob," said the captain dissuasively.

"That girl is an angel. I could never be happy

again as long as I lived if I did not save her," said Bob, impatiently.

"Well, Bob, I have been with you for years, and in some mighty close places; but I never knew you to swerve in the face of danger," returned the captain.

Then Bob cried, "I cannot bear for her to be in the hands of those fiends any longer. I will save her or die among them," and he drew his revolver and started toward the camp.

"You will not be alone, Bob," cried Ralph Tover, the youngest of the company, and all rushed down upon the Indians. But they were prepared for them this time, and fired at them with rifles and shot at them with arrows. But the rangers were moving so rapidly that the shot struck the hill behind them, and before the Indians could fire again they were upon them. With his revolver in his left hand, and the bridle thrown over the same, with which he guided his horse, and his right arm free, Bob Randon rushed headlong among them.

The Indians gathered closely around the girl, but he shot those down that were next to her with startling accuracy, and she, finding herself free, ran toward him with outstretched arms, like a child to its mother. With scarcely a perceptible check in his speed, he leaned over in his saddle and clasped the girl in his arm. At the same time he felt an arrow pierce that arm, but he heeded it not, and wheeled his horse, and burying his spurs in his sides, rushed from the place.

When the Indians saw this daring act, they scattered in every direction, trying to make their escape. Ralph Tover, who had been watching Bob, as soon as he saw him grasp the girl, followed closely after him, and as soon as they were out of danger, he leaped from his horse and took the girl from his arms. But when he saw her face, he cried out, "They have killed her! They have killed her!" But Bob said calmly, "She is not harmed; she has only fainted." And he untied a slicker from behind his saddle and threw it in the shade of a tuft of chaparrals, which the declining sun was throwing out toward the east. Ralph laid her gently on the pallet, while Bob knelt down and bathed her temples with water from his canteen.

The two men gazed upon her with troubled faces. Then there was a start, she opened her eyes—such brilliant brown eyes—and stared around her, and then they rested upon Bob Randon. A blush came to his cheeks; he thought he saw her smile on him—a sweet little smile.

The captain rode up, and seeing that the girl was safe, his eyes darted toward Bob, and he saw the arrow still sticking in his arm, the shield which had protected the girl from harm.

He sprang from his horse and, without a word, he grabbed the arm and drew the arrow out. A cry of pain came from Bob. He had until that moment forgotten that he was hurt. The blood flowed freely from the wound and ran down upon his hand.

The captain took his handkerchief, and, saturating it with water, wound it around the arm.

He then turned to the men who had just come up, and said, " We will not follow them any farther, nor bury those we have slain; they will make a good feast for the vultures and coyotes. The hack that we have taken from the Indians will do for you and the young lady to ride in, while Ralph Tover will drive," he said, turning to Bob, " and the rest of us will drive the horses."

So in a few hours they were traveling along the same way that they had passed over that morning. Bob Randon lay reclining in the bottom of the hack, while his fair companion sat near him on the seat. Sometimes he would look wonderingly at her; she was so beautiful; but her face was extremely pale, and there was a troubled expression about the eyes. She did not speak that evening, only in answer to their kind solicitations about her comfort. But that night, after supper, when they were all gathered around the fire, she surprised them by saying in the sweetest voice they had ever heard, "I have not told you all anything of my history, and you have been so thoughtful not to ask me any questions while I was too nervous to talk.

"My name is Susan Dalin, and my home is in Eastern Texas. About six months ago, my father, who was in declining health, was persuaded by a friend and neighbor, who had a ranch near Fort Davis, to go with him out there, as he was sure the climate would do him good. My father consented, and I begged him to take me with him. He tried to persuade me out of the notion. But I told him that I was romantic and wanted to experience some of the wild life of the West. But, really, I felt if he went away, I would never see him again. He did not get any better. The long trip across the plains did not seem to agree with him, and he gradually grew worse, until he died, about six months ago. The friend I spoke of before persuaded me to stay with him until he could get his business so arranged that we could return home. And we were on our way thither, when yesterday, about sunrise, we were attacked by the Indians. I think neither my friend nor the driver saw them until they fired, for I was asleep, and when I awoke the first thing I saw was my friend fallen backward in the hack. I fainted, and when I regained consciousness I was in the same hack, and two squaws sat on either side of me. I do not know what became of my friend and the driver. Only my trunk remained in the hack. It was open, and the squaws were examining its contents, when one that I supposed to be the chief rode up and said something to them that I did not understand. But they immediately closed the trunk, and I suppose he told them that I would need the things. The squaws were kind to me, but I could not understand anything they said. I was so lonesome that I thought I would go deranged, and this morning I was sitting in the hack dreaming over my wretchedness, when I heard the report of your guns. I thought somebody had attacked the Indians, and was just getting out of the hack to see what it was when I was seized by two powerful Indians and dragged out to where you first saw me. Oh, how glad I was to see some friendly faces ! I would have run towards you if they had not held me fast, although I knew it would have been certain death." At this she began to cry.

The men got up and moved restlessly about.

" Do not talk any more now," the captain said soothingly, " you need rest. You have been through a dreadful experience in the past few days. We have made a rude tent for you, where you can sleep, and where we have placed your trunk."

At this, he took her by the hand and led her to the door of the tent, and said, as he turned to leave, "If you need anything that it is in our power to bestow, you will make us happy by letting us know."

" I have all that my heart could desire ; and you all have been so kind to me," she replied earnestly.

If she had been a captive before, she was a princess now. The rough and sunburnt men walked lightly about for fear their footsteps would disturb her sleep; and would have all died together before harm could have come to her.

It is pleasing as well as pathetic, that the longer men are away from the society of women the more their respect and admiration for them increases. They watch them as if they were visitants from a better world. A word or smile from some fair face will make them happier than the wealth of worlds.

II.

THE next morning the rangers beheld the most beautiful sight that they had seen for years. She came out of the tent dressed in gay attire, which she wore instead of the mourning of the day before, because she knew it would please those noble souls better.

They gazed in wonderment upon the beautiful girl. She looked like some fairy queen in those wilds. The rose tints had returned to her cheeks, and that care-worn expression was gone from the eyes. She smiled sweetly as she bowed to each one of them. Then she saw Bob Randon lying on a pallet; his arm swelled dreadfully. She went and kneeled down beside him and took his hand in hers, " I am so sorry you suffer so on my account," she said passionately. Bob felt the tears come to his eyes, and he could only murmur: " I have done nothing; I have done nothing. Please say nothing about it."

Poor Bob, no wonder his heart beat violently; for no woman had smiled on him for many years. There was something in the warmth of her voice, something in the soft expression of her eyes, that thrilled him with a happiness he could not understand whenever she was near him.

They had not travelled far that morning, when they heard the muttering of distant thunder. All the morning the clouds had been creeping over from the west, and they were grim and threatening. The bull bats, those never-failing harbingers of a storm in the West, would swoop downward and almost strike the earth, screaming shrilly, and would then mount upward high against the heavy clouds.

" We are going to have a storm in a short time," said Ralph Tover, turning to his companions.

" Yes," returned Bob, " we shall have a storm before long; and it will be wind, rain, and hail, for I have never seen a cloud rise from that direction, and look like that, when we did not have a powerful rain."

Ralph alighted from the carriage and secured the curtains; and as they started on they noticed the men in front reining in their horses, and pulling on their slickers. The stillness of the air was painful; and they could hear an incessant roaring in the west. And every now and then the lightning strove to pierce the heavy atmosphere, but there would be only a pale momentary flash which could just be seen before it was gone. The thunder would crash in so suddenly and roll away to the south that it would cause the horses to jump, although they were looking for it. The men looked back with solemn faces upon the approaching storm. An arch of dark blue, as smooth as glass, rose in the north and reached over to the south. Along the top of the arch the jetty clouds boiled and worked in every direction; and travelling toward the south was a black rack which was frightful to look upon. Ralph Tover sat in silence, watching the horses walk slowly along. Susan Dalin and Bob Randon sat upon the hind seat, and gazed thoughtfully in front of them. They saw some antelopes moping about, their small bodies almost hidden in the oppressive gloom. The only cheerful thing that could be seen was a narrow strip of blue sky along the eastern horizon. Susan sat watching it until at last it was shut out by the sombre clouds.

"It looks now as if the sun could never shine out again," she said sadly, turning to Bob.

" Yes," he replied, " it looks as if the sun were for ever shut out from the world. But in a few hours the storm will be gone, and the sun will shine more brightly than before; the air will be purer and pleasanter, the grass, fresher and greener; and the flowers will shed their sweetest fragrance."

They were silent for a few moments; then he looked at her and asked quietly : " Are you afraid of storms, Miss Dalin? Do you think you will be frightened when this one strikes us ? "

"How could I be frightened with so many good and strong men to protect me," she replied, smiling sweetly, and there was a twinkle of mirth in her eyes.

"But we, who could save you from the Indians, would be helpless in the hands of the storm," he said solemnly.

But she could make no reply; for a few heavy drops spattered against the curtains for a few moments; then the wind struck them. It seemed as if it would overturn the hack; it whipped around it with

incessant din.   They did not speak to one another for
it would have been no use, for they could hardly hear
the thunder which pealed in continually.   Bob felt
Susan nestle close to him, and he took her hand in
his to reassure her of his presence; he knew how
lonesome and isolated she was in the fury of the
storm.   She sat still, gazing straight before her upon
the dismal scene; and as she saw the men who were
in front, her eyes grew moist with overwhelming sadness.   They had turned their backs to the wind and
rain; and their horses, with their heads lowered, stood
patiently, as if they knew it was their portion to take
the rain.   The water blew in undulating sheets, and
seemed to rise up and drench and redrench the men
with the icy drift.

But by and by the storm began to abate, and at last
the rain entirely ceased to fall.   The cloud moved
slowly over, leaving the clear blue sky behind; and its
edge grew brighter and brighter until the sun came
out in all his brilliancy.   A light fog rose from the
prairie, but quickly vanished away.   The rillets, that
were born of the storm, sparkled as they trickled
down the hillside and made a slight gurgle as they
glided over the gravels.   The horses were more lively,
and bounded forward with a buoyant force. The
prairies had put on a fresher coat of green.   As Susan
gazed out upon the beautiful world, her eyes sparkled
with delight, and she exclaimed, reaching out her
hands toward the plains:

"Oh! how beautiful is the world; and how sweet
does life seem to me now.   I can hardly believe it; it
does not seem real.   At this time yesterday my soul
seemed as dark, and my life as tumultuous, as the
storm that has just passed.   But now, like the storm,
it has passed rapidly away, and everything seems
more bright and joyful than before."

After the last white film of the cloud had disappeared in the east, the company came in sight of a
lofty peak that stood alone in the midst of the prairies.   "How lonesome that peak looks," said Susan,

" I wish we could pay it a visit. I feel that it would be conscious of our kindness."

" I will ask the captain when we come up with him and I know he will be willing to stop for a while for us to go up to the top of the peak. I would not have you to miss it for anything. It is the most wonderful view you ever saw," replied Bob, thinking what a sweet girl his companion must be to feel compassion for the loneliness of an inanimate thing.

In a short while they came up with the rest of the party, and Bob made known his desires to the captain, but received the reply, " Yes, Bob, we will stop for the young lady to go upon the mountain; but you are not able to accompany her yourself."

" Oh, yes, I can," replied Bob eagerly," it is only my arm that is hurt. It will do me good to walk up there."

" Very well, you can do as you like," returned the captain carelessly. But when he was alone with his companions, he said:

"I never saw a boy so smitten as Bob Randon. It would do him more harm to keep him away from that girl a moment than anything in the world."

So in an hour Susan and Bob, accompanied by several of the men, were picking their way up the peak ; and when they reached the top both were exhausted; and there was but one tree upon the peak, a low bushy hackberry, which had grown in a crevice of the mighty rocks. Here their companions left them to rest in the shade. A flush of health and excitement was upon Susan's lovely features, which Bob had never seen there before. She sat down and gazed upon the entrancing scene, wholly unconscious that her companion was lying on a big rock, with his head resting upon one of his hands, watching her in the deepest thought. They seemed to be in the centre of a great arena; and the mountains which surrounded them were almost hid in the skyey haze. They had been sitting in silence for some time when Susan said thoughtfully, without looking at her companion : " I

4

wonder if the Indians have appreciated the beauties of this grand picturesqueness in the many ages that they have lived here."

"No doubt of it," replied Bob, "I have just been weaving a kind of romance of my own while you were looking absently away. I was thinking that probably on these very rocks have sat the dusky youths and maidens and plighted their vows, and as they gazed upon the wondrous scene, their souls expanded and flowed into each other."

Their companions returned at this instant, and they all slowly descended the mountain.

As the days passed by, Bob lounged in the hack while Susan sat near him and related pleasant stories for his diversion. She told him of her happy home, and how she loved music and art; and how she longed to get home again to her piano and drawings. Then they would look out upon the slightly ruffled sea of grass into which the far-off hills jutted out like promontories.

A new life had come to Bob Randon, a life which he was not conscious of. With that sweet girl near him where he could gaze upon her face every day, he felt that he was living in a dream. Sometimes he would lie with his eyes closed, and would be so happy that he would open them and look at her before he could realize that he was not dreaming. He had been with her but a few days, but it seemed like he had known her all his life ; so rapidly does love grow, it becomes so powerful in a few days that even death cannot overcome it. Bob had reached that degree of love. But he had been so extremely happy that he had not thought of how he would live when Susan was gone; how lonely and wretched his life would be, for he could never live contented without her. It seemed to come to him suddenly just as the darkness was settling over the plains on the last night before they reached Fort Concho where she was to leave them for her home. He had been riding alone with her all day, for his arm had improved so much that he was able to drive. But she had been unusually vivacious, and attractive, and he had thought of nothing else. But now his soul was filled with anguish. He knew he could not sleep, and begged his comrades to let him stay on guard. He walked violently to and fro; and would stop now and then and look at the tent, wondering how it could hold all the happiness of his life. If any one had been listening, they would have heard him repeating: "Bob Randon, you are a rough fellow; no woman could ever love you; you could never ask her to marry you, for if she accepted you, it would only be from pity, and the kindness of her heart; yes, you must be contented to suffer the rest of your days, for she could never love you." With this decision, he lay down when the night was far spent, and tried to sleep.

The next day Susan and Bob were alone. For several hours they had been travelling on in silence. Both seemed to be buried in profound thought. Moved by some irresistible impulse, Bob looked at her. She was looking at him. Something in the expression of her eyes emboldened him. For without taking time to think how it would sound, he said, his whole soul in his eyes and voice:

"It seems so strange, Miss Dalin, that I have hoped that all would go well until we reached Fort Concho and I would be so happy when I knew that you were safe on your way home. But now I believe it will be the darkest day of my life when you leave us."

She made no reply, but turned her face from him, and presently he discovered that she was sobbing quietly. A great uneasiness crept over him.

"O, Miss Dalin, you must forgive me if I have said anything rude that would hurt your feelings. I am not used to the society of ladies; I do not know how to talk to them," he cried, with anguish in his voice.

"You have said nothing to hurt my feelings," she replied earnestly. "I was so surprised that you were thinking of the same thing that I was. I was wondering how I could leave you without crying."

A great hope came to Bob Randon, such a hope as can come to a man but once in his life.

" You cannot regret leaving me," he said eagerly. "I have imagined that you were unhappy with us; and were longing to reach Fort Concho. I thought you were so lonesome in these wilds, with a company of tanned, unshaven, and unpolished men."

" I have been very happy with you all," she replied, earnestly, "and I was so wretched last night I could not sleep, for thinking how lonely I would be on my way home, without any one in the world to care for me."

" I cannot bear to see you go away alone," cried Bob. "Will you let me go with you? Will you let me be with you all the time?"

" O, I would be so happy," she replied, almost pleadingly. "It would be more happiness than I ever expected to have in this life. I shall be alone in the world without you," she continued. "I have neither father nor mother, brother nor sister, only a few distant relatives who take no interest in me."

" But," said Bob, reflectively, "I am such a rough man you cannot love me well enough to marry me. It is only because you feel that you are indebted to me. It all comes of your angelic heart. You would regret it in the course of time."

" Do you know," she said, smiling, and looking up at him archly, "when I first saw you that day as I regained consciousness, I thought you were the most handsome man whom I had ever seen. You looked so noble and grand that I have loved you ever since."

He clasped her to his bosom, and kissed her again and again. When they looked around them again, the men in front were just mounting a hill; and a short distance to one side was a flock of antelopes, and some of them were looking bewitchingly at them.

When the rangers bade Susan and Bob good-bye, the big tears trickled down the cheeks of rough and sunburnt men; and when they reached their home,

Bob could not be made more happy than he was before when he discovered that he had won a great heiress. Susan made him the hero of her little world; and Bob thinks his wife the sweetest little woman in Texas.

THE WATER-SPOUT.

ALMOST everybody in Western Texas remembers the great water-spout of 1882 which broke upon the head of the Concho river and rushed downward, a mighty wall of roaring, seething waters, working death and destruction as it went. It rolled swiftly downward where the banks were steep and the course of the river narrow; but where there were necks made by bends in the river, or the bottom widened out into level fertile valleys, the waters expanded and swept along houses, families, and stock of every kind. Heavy rains had fallen upon the heads of all the rivers, the tributaries of the Colorado, while there had not been a shower lower down. When this water, increased by the wave of the water-spout, reached the Colorado and spread over its valleys, the devastation was terrible. The settlers went to bed the evening before, little dreaming that they were lying down to their last sleep of life. It was a dry time; no rain had fallen for several weeks. Lightning had been seen for several evenings far back in the west, but that was nothing uncommon. Without a warning, in the dead of night, the merciless waters swept over them. Awakened by the unearthly din, they could not understand what was upon them, only conscious that some awful danger was near, which made the death the more terrible. Some of the old pioneers who escaped said that they had heard the yell of the Indians amid the groans of the dying and the noise of the slaughter, but were not terrified as at the roar of this wall of water. The next day one could stand upon the edge of the water of the Colorado river and just see the dim outline of the misty shore on the other side. All the towns along the Concho and Colorado rivers were threatened, and many suffered great damages. Nearly the entire town of San Angelo was washed away; and some of its oldest inhabitants, who had lived many long and peaceful years in this land of sunshine and dry, cloudless weather, found a grave beneath the merciless stream.

On the evening previous to the overflow mentioned above, a cowboy was jogging along leisurely down the Colorado bottom, wending his way to where there was to be a round-up the next day. The small pony he rode was a careless-going, never-tiring Spanish, and he drove several extra horses and the pack horse carrying his " grub," cooking utensils, and blankets. As night came on, he stopped, built a fire, unsaddled the horses and took them out to the high ground and hoppled them where the grass was good; for the prairie dogs had picked the ground bare in the valley. Little did he think that he was taking more pains for the safety of the faithful animals than for himself. After eating supper, he spread down his blankets, and putting his slicker and boots under his head, he listened for a while to the singing of the mocking bird, the howling of the coyote, and cries of other denizens of the bottom, then fell asleep.

He was startled from sleep by a roaring as of a thousand cyclones, and in his bewilderment he thought a storm was approaching, and quickly drew on his boots and slicker. In the mean time he glanced up at the sky. It was a clear, tranquil summer night. What could it be ? He had fought the Indians and kept his nerves amid their hideous yells ; he had pushed his horse without a tremor at full speed adown declivities and over rocky hills and across dangerous dog-towns ; when on the trail he had heard the tramp of thousands of cattle in stampede ; but he was never frightened as he was for a moment as he listened to this strange unaccountable thunder in a calm and cloudless night. He was struck by some mighty force and whirled around and tossed about like a feather. The cold water penetrated his clothes, and sometimes he felt himself suffocating and thought it all over. But somehow his slicker seemed to keep him afloat. He was a good swimmer, and as he collected his thoughts he saw his situation and fought for his life as only a Texas cowboy can fight. He was carried on swiftly for some moments, but they seemed so many hours to him. The current struck him violently against a floating object, which stunned him for a while, and the attraction only held him to it. He reached out and felt a log, and getting hold of a limb he climbed upon it. He could see that it was a large elm, for the moon poured her peaceful silvery light down upon the troubled waters. He crawled to the large branches where he would be in less danger of being swept off. Once the log was sucked into a whirlpool and turned round and round and over, and he clung to it with a drowning grip, and came up again shivering and dripping ; and he lay back in a fork, utterly exhausted, and gazed up at the quiet moon, so far away and safe from all danger. The quiet heavens tantalized him. The polar star and the dipper hung beautifully in the north, and a brilliant comet threw its bright red streamers across them as it followed the sun in his course around the opposite side of the earth, while the pale milky-way engirdled the twinkling vault, and the raging waters, painted with the glistening whiteness, fading in the distance, looked like mist.

The summer night was short, which was a blessing. The comet which, in company with the moon and stars, kept him company through the night, faded away along the eastern horizon, and the dawn took its place. As the dawn glowed with dead gold light upon the boiling, rolling river, he saw that he must be a quarter of a mile from the bank. He was not in the middle of the river, and thanked his stars that he was not. The sights on all sides were terrifying. The current rose in mountains and sank in chasms, bearing swiftly downward the evidence of wrecked towns and peace-

ful homes.   A piano floated by, then a billiard table.
Box houses sailed by entirely whole and only half sub-
merged, and only the floor or roofs of others.   The
sun arose.   The cowboy was floating through a land
that looked strange to him.   Doubtless he had passed
over it before, but it was deformed now.   It was many
yards to the shore, and the current was swift and
dangerous between him and it.   Clumps of live oaks
stood here and there on the banks, and the tinted hills
lay serenely in the distance; and the paradise bird
flew over him, screaming as if terrified by this stormy
enemy breaking in upon its quiet.

He glanced up the river; the top of a house was
visible, and it came swooping down with frightful
rapidity.   It attracted his attention because he thought
he saw a white handkerchief fluttering at a window.
For it was a two-storey house which sank into the
water up to the upper floor.   As it neared him, he saw
a lady standing at a window, waving a handkerchief,
evidently hoping to attract the attention of anybody
that might be on the shore.   He knew that she was
frightened and needed help.   But what could he do
for her?   Doubtless she was alone and lonesome like
himself.   For he was beginning to long to see a
human being again.   And would not the house be
safer than the log?   This passed through his mind in
a moment, and, hazardous as it was, he plunged into
the current to try to swim to the house and catch on
as it floated by.   He missed the distance and would
not have reached the house before it was gone, had
not the current borne him down so much faster,
and he was dashed against a corner and whirled
around almost senseless, and he felt the water sucking
him downward, and he caught a glimpse of the
window, and he clutched it with one hand, but he felt
his strength going as the boiling water beside the
floating building sucked him under it.   He felt two
soft hands clasp his wrist and draw him up until he
reached the sill with his other hand; he then drew
himself into the window.

As he stepped into the room, his feet splashed in the water, and he saw that everything was wet in the room. He looked around to take in the situation. The water was about a foot deep on the floor, and, as the current tossed the house about, it ran from first one side to the other. The furniture, toilet articles of a lady's room, lay scattered in confusion about the room. And on a centre table, securely placed beside the window, the girl was seated, and upon it she had stood to wave the handkerchief. He gazed into her face. She was pale, and uneasiness was depicted upon her features; but she was firm—prepared for any fate; he saw that. He saw that her garments were saturated, everything was wet, and he was wet too. But it was his nature to give a cheerful aspect to everything, and, with all the carelessness and gayety of the cow-camp, he said:

"This is not very easy riding, I am sure. Our horse is not sure-footed, and is liable to get his legs tangled and fall and roll over us and put out daylight."

He said this so comically that the girl smiled in spite of herself.

"Do you think there is the slightest chance to escape?" she asked, looking anxiously at him.

"I do," he replied, and there was not a doubt manifested in his looks. "If no drift should strike me, I could swim to land, although I might drift down a mile or so before I reached it." He noticed that she was shivering, and he felt chilled himself, Although the sun was shining fiercely, the water was icy, and the mist that rose from it was chilling.

He looked out at the window and surveyed the situation. He looked up the river; a massive drift of logs, planks and roofs of houses, that reached nearly half across the river, was drifting down upon them. They were not in the swiftest of the current and were moving slowly, and for that reason the edge of the drift would overtake them soon, and there would be no chance of escape. He looked down the river. Far down the misty plain a neck of land with several live oaks on it, reached far out into the river, making a bay of almost quiet water, and they would pass near the edge of the current. Here was the only chance. He decided on the moment; and, turning to his companion, he said, " The only chance for us to save ourselves is to swim."

"But I do not know how to swim," she replied.

"I did not suppose you did; but are you willing to do what I suggest?"

"I am," she replied, readily.

Removing his slicker and boots, he took a quilt and tore it into shreds, and bound her securely to his back, and his skill at tying down beeves came into play; and without any hesitation he plunged again into the current.

He swam heroically, but the current swept him downward with frightful swiftness and often took his breath away. He could not see if he was drifting past the neck of land. But he pressed on, buffeting the current, although he seemed forced back as far as he had moved himself forward. Almost suddenly he found himself in almost quiet water. And as he swam he could see at times the trees reaching out into the river, and he knew he had not passed his harbor. But the trees were several hundred yards away, and he was nearly spent; could he ever reach them? He was in despair. Then he thought the water forced out by the current would run round in a circle and would pass near the bank. And he exerted himself no longer, but just managed to keep afloat. Ages, it seemed to him, he floated down before he found that he was borne around near the land. When he saw that the water would carry him no nearer, he put his strength to the test once more. But it would not comply; his limbs quivered and he felt strangely weak. Not even the trees, a short distance away upon a pleasant hill, could put fresh life into his limbs, but they caused him to push forward again, and his knees struck the ground, and he stood up. The ground was firm, for the grass was still upon it, and though the water was nearly up to his neck he stopped to rest, and asked his companion, with a faint voice, if she were alive. When she answered him with a firm voice, "Yes, more alive than you."

This cheered him, and he waded on slowly till he crawled up the hill to a safe distance, and reaching into his pocket he drew out his long knife and released his precious burden, and sank, completely exhausted, to the earth.

He lay for a long time without saying a word, watching the girl, who sat near him, looking anxiously at him. There was a light of thankfulness in her eyes, and he thought from her looks that she felt grateful to him, but she expressed it not in words.

When he was rested, he arose and said, "Suppose we walk up to the trees on the hilltop and see if we can see a house." When they reached the trees, they saw a cozy cottage embowered with live oaks in a valley to the north.

"We will walk down to that house and ask for something to eat," he said. "They cannot refuse us."

It proved to be a warm walk; for the summer sun shone down fiercely, strangely in contrast to the icy river which still roared in their ears.

They were received kindly at the cottage, and the good man and his wife supplied the waifs with a fresh wardrobe. Our cowboy saw nothing more of the young lady until the next day, when she sent for him. He found her seated languidly in the parlor. He started, for he had not taken particular notice of her face before. She was a grand woman, this queen of the water-spout, whom he had found alone in her floating castle. And he stood admiring her until she spoke.

"I am very uneasy about my father," she began. "Mother was away from home the night the river rose, and I am thankful she was. I was sleeping in an upper room and father below.   I am afraid he did not escape.   Do you know Colonel Etherton ? "

" I have often seen him and know him well by character."

" Well, I am his daughter ? "

" I am glad if I have been of service to you," he said.

He knew Colonel Etherton to be a great ranchman and land-owner, and, if dead, it would be a great loss to the country.

" Do you know how far we are from father's ranch?" she asked.

" I do not know for certain.   But we are several days' ride."

" Oh, I would be so happy if I knew father escaped !

" I can procure a horse and go and see, and if he is alive, he will be glad to hear that you are safe."

" Oh, I will always be so thankful if you will ! And he will come immediately after me."

The next morning early the cowboy started on his ride.   When he reached Colonel Etherton's ranch, he found that the Colonel escaped, but he and his wife were nearly distracted at the loss of their only child. When the cowboy broke to them the good news, the mother wept, and the father grasped the young man's hand and declared that he was the noblest man alive; and, turning to his wife, said, "We must send word to Fred Uland that Kate is safe ; for he has been in consolable."

At this the cowboy turned pale ; and a strange feeling of desolation crept over him that he had never felt before.   He knew Fred Uland well; had run cattle with him and slept under the same blanket. But Fred was rich, and far superior to him in good looks.   And an indescribable hatred for his old friend took possession of his heart, but he knew not why. He could not be in love with the girl.

Later on, he learned that Fred Uland and Kate Etherton were engaged ; and Fred Uland came and shook hands with him and said that he was the best boy in the world, and took his departure down the river after his betrothed.

He saw her once again. She was at a picnic. He stood and watched her for a long while. She was so grand and beautiful as she, smiling, looked up at Fred Uland, and he turned away with an unconquerable hatred for that man, although he knew he should not ; for Fred was a good fellow, and had always been kind to him. And probably she would be happier with Fred than with him; for he had the means to furnish her with all the pleasures of life, while he was but a poor unknown cowboy. He never saw her more. He looked not upon his rescue of her from the drift on the river as anything heroic ; but, contented at the result of the whole thing, he went back to his old life of work. And as he has passed through this story without a name, so are his name and his deed unknown outside of his camp.

ENOIS AND UELA.

ENOIS was not his real name; Stephen Brakley was what he was first named; but, while a small boy at school, his teacher, a scholar from Massachusetts, called him Enois, a contraction of a Greek word, because of his habitual thoughtfulness. And his father, a finished classical scholar, thinking the name pretty, and being well pleased with its import, had kept it up; and it came to be that he was known to many by no other name than Enois.

His father and mother had moved to the west when he was a very little boy, and this family, different from most that came to settle in the west, brought with them a large library. For Mr. Brakley could not leave his beloved books, and he felt that he would need their company more than ever in an uninhabited country. As soon as they had built a rude house, the books were taken from the boxes in which they were packed, and set up.

Enois engaged in many of the occupations of the west.   He could not be called a farmer, although with patient oxen he broke many acres of the virgin sod; he was not strictly a cowboy, although he had followed that life until he was an expert with the lasso; he was not a shepherd, although he had worked at that dreamy business upon the verdant prairies and the tinted hills and beside the limpid streams.   He was a dreamer; yes, a student, in a land devoid of colleges, where the few inhabitants lived almost a wild life through winter and summer, and had no higher thoughts and aspirations than cattle and horses, and had almost, or entirely, forgotten the refinements of society.

In his leisure hours, his retirement was with the books in the small room built of hewn oak logs and roof made of shingles of the same wood.   Here he gained a smattering of the ancient classics, and read English literature with tireless avidity.   When he looked upon the verdant prairies, adorned here and there with clusters of live oaks that kept their coat of bright green untarnished by autumnal gloom, or withering frost, or terrific blizzards; and the level valleys beside the winding streams, skirted with pecans, where the horses and cattle grazed in dreamy contentment—with scarcely a sight of an abode of man —he thought of Milton's grand description of Eden, and a world first inhabited by man.   As he fed his oxen it brought to mind Virgil's description of rural life in the Bucolics, and his beautiful mention of the portion of the produce that should go to the deserving steers.   He read the sermons of Spurgeon, and imagined himself seated in the Tabernacle, London, listening to the voice of that wondrously noble man.   He mused upon all that is noble, beautiful, and grand in poetry, and romance for him threw a glamour over the western wilds. The cowboys with overalls of long hair, and rawhide lasso, dashing wildly over the prairies by day, and sleeping in tents or under cliffs by night, brought to mind the sacred story of people dressed in the tawny furs of beasts, who lived in caves of the earth. To his companions in the camp, and to all the settlers around, he was an incomprehensible mystery. Though they idolized him, they could not understand him, and thought him peculiar in mind.

One winter, Enois, with many other cowboys, was camped far away from home to ride lines on the Pecan Bayou. One dreary day it rained all the morning, and in the evening it turned suddenly cold by a norther blowing up, and the rocks which cover the ridges along this stream were glazed with a slippery crust of ice. While Enois was pushing his horse recklessly down a slant, the noble animal slipped on a broad rock and was precipitated violently down the slope, throwing Enois against the ground and rolling over him. When his companions rode up, they found Enois pale and cold, lying insensible, his handsome brow surrounded by the icicled grass. They saw that he was dangerously injured; and, taking him gently up, one rode with him in his arms many miles to the nearest house, while another went for a doctor, and the others followed on, looking anxiously at the limp form of their endeared companion to catch any sign of life there. They laid him upon a soft bed in a warm room, richly furnished. With open hospitality, the good people of the house placed everything at the disposal of the cowboys, and their injured comrade.

The house to which they took Enois was owned by one Mr. Malton. This man had come to Western Texas in Indian times; and, like the feudal barons of old, having the choice of the whole country, he had taken an admirable situation for a home and ranch at the confluence of two streams. He built a spacious and formidable stone residence of the rock quarried from the neighboring hills. He opened a rich valley farm, and surrounded it with a stone fence; and the ridges that lay on the west, fit only for grazing lands, he fenced with wire, and thousands of horses, cattle, and sheep grazed upon his lands and came down to drink from the Bayou and its tributaries. With his many employés he took a stand against the Indians, and did much to rid the country of those foes. And at the time of this story he owned one of the most desirable places in Western Texas, and he deserved it.

When Enois came to life, he felt perfectly easy in body and mind, as if he would like to lie down and sleep forever, all seemed so peaceful and dreamy as one in a morphic stupor. His eyes rested upon the pictures on the walls and the fine furniture. This was not a cow-camp. Where could he be? What had happened? His memory was a blank. He could not remember where he had been or what he had been doing for many days. He had never felt so strangely at ease before in his life.

The door gently opened, and a young girl came stealthily into the room. His eyes rested upon her, but he did not move. Her open countenance was turned upon him. He had never seen such a face before. He had often brought before his mind the face of his ideal of a woman. This ideal of his was different from any woman he had ever seen in cast of features and in ways. She was the embodiment of perfection as imagined in his own mind; more beautiful and good than the characters drawn by the poets and novelists. The face before him was the perfection of his ideal. There was a play of mirth and seriousness blended in natural sweetness upon her features. Golden curls played idly upon her broad white forehead. As she moved her lovely head, the golden richness trembled in wavy sheen. She looked at him for a moment, and went out as quietly as she entered. And in the confusion of his brain he thought that he had passed that dreaded bourn and seen his divine perfection of beauty and love in the summer home beyond, and then returned to this land of winter and death.

One of his comrades came in and spoke to him of how glad he was to see that he was coming back to life,

The physician came. Enois was not dangerously injured. He was badly bruised, and his brain had received an awful shock. It would be many days before he could be about.

The cowboys took it time-about nursing him; and it was pathetic how anxiously they watched over him and inquired of the people of the house how they thought he was.

One evening as he lay musing, soft music came to him from some part of the building. It was a lady's voice, accompanied by a piano. It had been a long time since he had heard such music, and his weary soul drank the refreshing strains; and it did him more good than any physics. Who could be the performer? She must be the vision that he saw on the day that he was hurt. He got out of bed and dressed himself, and walked out into the hall. Through a half-open door he saw that head of sunny curls, and a divine expression was upon her fair open face in harmony with the transporting melody of the song. He softly entered, and stood watching her, and she played for some time before she discovered his presence.

" You should not be up," she said.

" Your singing inspired me, and I could not remain in the room."

She quit playing, and he returned to his room, musing on Tennyson's Maud, and her head sunning over with curls. Nowhere in ancient or modern poetry and romance could he remember any description of woman that could be applied to her, and he called her Uela because of her sunny curls and he found later that the name suited her disposition; and she was the sunlight upon his dreary life.

He inquired of one of the men about the place who she was, and learned that she was Mr. Malton's daughter Eva, and the mistress of his home; for her mother was dead. Her father had sent her east to school until she finished her education; and now she was the most accomplished young lady in the west.

After this, as he lounged about the house, he list-

5

ened to her singing and playing, and the tender music in league with the radiant beauty of her face and the sheen of her sunny curls, and above all, his unbounded love for her; and when she turned her face full upon him, it enraptured his spirit as when the Spirit quiets the troubled soul. Beautiful thoughts only were visitants of his mind; and wholly lovely seemed life. He felt the tears come to his eyes from sheer happiness, and he would that he could always live thus. He wondered if she loved any man. He thought that he would be satisfied only to be conscious that she was free, even if she could never be near to him.

Very pleasantly passed the long winter evenings. Uela's sunny disposition made everybody glad about her. Enois discovered that she had read much and was acquainted with all his favorite authors. He was always thoughtful and melancholy; she light and joyful. He had come to love her so that he had forgotten all else but looking upon her face and listening to her voice. Sometimes he felt that she cared for him; that she admired him he knew, but then he was nothing but a poor cowboy, while she was the daughter of one of the most wealthy men in the country. He could see that Mr. Malton did not like his being so much with his daughter, and as soon as he was well Enois returned home.

As he rode homeward over hills and prairies, it seemed mysterious how things had changed for him since last he rode over the same way. His life seemed enriched by some latent happiness; yet it made him ill at ease, for it was not yet in his possession. A bright face crowned with many curls ever seemed to smile benignantly on him, and he thought of her as he read of heroines in poetry and romance; but all pen-pictures were blank and dead. All that is voluptuous in languid Southern beauty, Uela possessed. But above all to him was her power to make sunshine and mirth wherever she might be.

Many times Enois called at the great stone house

on the Bayou to see Uela, and was graciously received. But one day he called and found that all was changed for him. He had known all along that Mr. Malton spurned him, and considered him wholly unworthy of his daughter's love. And this evening no one met him at the door, and as he stopped in the hall he heard a stranger's voice and Uela's in one of the adjoining rooms.

Mr. Malton appeared and said, " My daughter has company to-day, and can receive no visitors."

But Enois remained until after supper, where he had a good look at the stranger. He was a man far advanced in years. Brilliant diamonds shone as he moved about. His hands were large and white ; his face showed no feeling, but was always calm. But Enois detected beneath that quiet exterior the soul of a devil ; and an unconquerable dislike for him arose in his breast.

Enois went to his faithful friend, one of Mr. Malton's hired men, whom he had asked that day about Uela; from whom he learned that Mr. Malton's guest was a banker in some northern city who had come out west for his health.

" Mr. Malton is stuck on him because he thinks he is rich ; which I doubt," the man went on ; " and he intends to marry his daughter to him, though he knows she despises him."

Enois turned away. He had often heard Mr. Malton express himself on this subject. He desired his daughter to marry a man wealthy and highly honored, who could raise her into the social world. With only this in view, he had taken great pains in, and spent much money on, her education. He could not bear to think that she might wed one of the cowboys of the neighborhood.

The man slapped him on the shoulder and said good-naturedly : " Old boy, Mr. Malton and the old dude are going to Baird to-day. You ride off and stay until they are gone and then return and make love to Miss Eva. I know she loves you. Don't let old man Malton's notions be in the way. Beat that old scamp at all hazards. It would be too bad for him to take away the prettiest, sweetest, and best girl in Western Texas."

Oh, how Enois loved that man just then! And his soul yearned to be with Uela alone once more.

He rode away to the top of one of the hills near by. Autumn veiled the hills on the north in sombre haze. It had been nearly a year since he first saw Uela.

By-and-by he saw the carriage drive off, and he returned. The people of the place were all about their work, and he found Uela alone in the bright parlor. She seemed so glad that he had returned. He poured out his longing soul to her in soft love words, of which he was master.

She clung to him and almost cried in despair, " O, Enois, my handsome, my incomparable Enois, why did you suffer yourself to fall into such an infatuation? I thought I would be the only one to suffer. Oh, how I love you! But I have known all the time that you could never be anything to me; for father would never forgive me for loving you if he knew it. And oh, how I have striven against my love. But then I thought you did not care for me. But now if you are to suffer, how can I bear it!"

" Nothing can ever separate us unless you will it," he said. " If your father objects because I am a poor cowboy, come, we will flee to-day."

" It can never be. I have already promised father to marry that man, and the wedding is set for Christmas week. Oh, how I hate that man."

" I would rather slay you with my own hand than that you should marry that fiend. And then he will take you away up north. How can you leave Texas?"

" It will break my heart to leave my beloved home, the clear blue skies, the purple hills, the land of my girlhood, and I have never known another. And my fair Texas boy, oh, how I suffer to have to give him up!"

" Come with me at once. I will make you happy whatever comes. We will have a cozy little home in this fair land of our youths which we both love so well, and that foreigner can never harm us."

" Go, go, my Enois, there is a life of usefulness before you. Work for the honor of our country. You have the talents for anything, while I must drag out a life of misery in a foreign land. But let us be friends forevermore."

The world, which had been so beautiful to Enois through a romantic glamour, seemed blank and uninspiring now; and the hills and valleys over which his boyish feet had trod, gladdened him not as once they did, as they decked themselves in the wild flowers of the May. He moped about in gloomy abstraction; and he looked up not at the blue sky with eyes dreamy with musings of romance and song. He had no object in life; and as he mused in the shadows of the evening, of that beautiful creature who had charmed his life, and brought before his mind her face, and realized what was gone from his life at the loss of her, his anguish became unbearable. But when he considered what a pleasingly grand reflection her friendship had thrown upon his dreary life, he felt thankful that he had known such a being. He never received any reliable tidings of her. He never knew whether she was happy or not. But rumors, which he hoped were not true, came to him that she was an innocent victim of desertion, sin, and shame. And he could not realize that she was the cast-off wife of another, when he would have died for her. Why was it decreed that they should not live together in their love in the fair land of the south? And those who knew them both felt that sin was upon the earth, that two so well fitted for each other, and so beautiful in their lives, should have been separated.

LANCIUM AND HECLEA

A POEM OF WESTERN TEXAS.

BOOK I.

I.

DAYS PRIMEVAL.

IN days primeval the fierce Indians lived
In their way in this, then wild, land of ours;
And, unrestrained, roamed where'er they willed,
And slew the antelope and buffalo,
Or in the wigwams spent their worthless days.
With motley paint upon their high cheek-bones,
And fire defiance glaring in their eyes,
They held their war-dance, and their hideous cries
Arose and died upon the fresh, pure air.

In days primeval grazed the buffaloes
In countless numbers o'er this land of ours.
Their short, monotonous low floated up
From morn till night upon the prairie air;
They cut deep paths down to the crystal pools,
And there the Indians many of them slew.
Their bones, in piles, lay bleaching in the sun—
Crude monuments that told a silent tale
To other eyes.

II.

THE COWBOY'S REIGN.

Then there were driven forth
Vast herds of cattle, that spread o'er the plains,
And fed, knee-deep, in the rank, waving grass,
And rough cowboys inhabited the wilds,
And suffered untold hardships in the camp.
Some lived in tents, some built rude sheds,
With ledges of rocks upon the northern sides.
They were always in danger—ever armed,
They swiftly crossed the prairies on their lines.
The prairie-dogs awoke the desert calm
With shrill, short bark as they rode through the
      towns;
The bold coyotes wandered forth in droves—
In savage beauty sought their prey by day;
The tawny badgers toddled here and there,
Or burrowed great holes with their frightful claws
Down to the snug dens of the prairie-dogs,
And mercilessly ate the occupants;
The antelopes grazed in the dreamy dells,
Or looked about them with bewitching grace,
Or glided swiftly o'er the tinted hills.

They were good-hearted men as ever lived,
These cowboys, with their tanned and sunburnt cheeks;
But no fair face scarce ever met their eyes,
And they almost forgot the ties of home.
But an attachment grew among them then
As strong as can exist 'tween man and man.
In after years, when all their lives were changed,
Drawn by the memory of once loneliness,
When they endured the same hardships together,
Were joined in friendship that could ne'er be snapt
By length of time, or civilization's rule.

III.

THE EMIGRANTS.

Next, poor men, with their families, moved out,
To till the soil and live upon the yields;
They brought their little herds of horse and cow.

Among the emigrants bound for the West
Was a poor farmer.   Warder was his name.
He had long struggled with stern poverty;
But there seemed no escape from his hard lot;
And he came to try the free Western lands.
His family was composed of only four—
His wife and three small children—two were boys.
The oldest was a girl, but twelve years old,
Sweet Heclea, the meek heroine of our tale.
Soft blue eyes had she, that dilated as
She gazed in wonder o'er the broad expanse;
Bright golden tresses played about her brow,
When fanned by the soft breezes from the south.

As the long string of wagons and of herds
Across the prairie serpentinely moved,
A matchless panorama was revealed.
The blue hills rose in broken chains along
The north, extending to the south, with here
And there, cut off, an isolated peak.
All were delighted with the glorious land,
And hoped here to escape the tyrant's rule.
Now, here was Freedom's undisputed realm,
And Liberty's mild reign was over all!
The air was pure and boundless as the heavens;
The prairies lay untenanted as far
In all directions as the eye could see;
No smoke curled upward on the bracing air
From residences in the silent woods.
Could it be wrong, could any one object,
For them to settle here and live in peace?

Broad, fertile valleys, ornate with clear pools,
With sparkling streamlets, and with gurgling springs,
And shady live-oak groves, where they could build,
Smiled, beckoning them to come and dwell on them.

It was in autumn when the emigrants,
Aweary with long travel, pitched their tents
Among the woods that skirted the blue hills,
Where here and there a limpid streamlet ran
From fountains gushing up among the hills.
Along these streams decided they to build.
They had no money, but no difference ;
For it was many miles to any town
Where they could have got lumber, had they tried.
The men into the woods proceeded with their axes,
Where was no sign of woodman's axe, and cut
House logs and sawed board timber from straight
      trees ;
For all was anxious hurry in the camps—
The dread of winter that was coming on.
Worked they upon their houses ceaselessly:
The women, children, doing all they could
To help the men upon their mutual work.

IV.

A SCARE.

One day some hunters passed the men at work.
They were returning from the West, where they
Had been to slay the buffaloes for their hides.
Their wagons were high piled with woolly hides
That had been torn from luscious meat, that lay
To be consumed by vultures and the wolves.
These hunters cried, " Flee ! flee ! or all are lost.
The Indians are now coming in their rage.
An awful fight has taken place just back
Upon the Colorado but last night ;

And many men and women have been killed,
And scalped, and all their property destroyed."
Both fathers, brothers, hastened to their homes,
And told the women and the children all.
A great uneasiness, fears too deep for tears
Fell upon every heart, and no one spoke.
That night was one to be remembered by
The settlers for the horrors of its hours:
The fires were put out, and no lights were lit,
There was no sound of habitation heard;
The tents were hidden by the moonless night.
All was so quiet, that the settlers hoped
The savages would miss them as they passed.
The women, breathless, caught each passing sound,
The murmur of the restless winds they thought
The stealthy tread of moccasined savages.
In one small tent the occupants slept not,
It was the nearest tent to the dim road
Where they supposed the Indians would go by,
And it would be the first to be attacked.
Mrs. Warder and her daughter Heclea
Sat motionless and peered into the night.
The screech-owl cried with accents tremulous
And the sad sounds the frightened watchers took
For signals for the murderous onset.
They started as they heard the coyotes howl
As if in revelry about the camps.

V.

A VISITOR.

The morning came and went, and about noon
A solitary horseman hove in sight.
He left the road and rode up to the tent
And asked if he could get his dinner there.
"Yes," Mrs. Warder replied, pleased with his looks.
He was a cowboy out-and-out.   He drew
His overalls off and came into the tent.

" Have you this morning from the river come ? "
Asked Mr. Warder. " Yes," the man replied.
" Have you been fighting Indians any there ? "
The cowboy shook his head. " Why so ? " he asked.
" Some hunters told me yesterday there was
A band of Indians on the Colorado,
And they had many of the white folks killed."
The young man smiled, and said, " It is a sell.
No Indians have been in for these two years."
" How could they treat us so ? " Mrs. Warder cried.
" It could have been no benefit to them."
" I reckon that they thought to have some fun."
The honest cowboy was a friend indeed,
To ease the minds of the scared settlers.
With boundless admiration Heclea gazed
Into the countenance of the young man
Who talked so pleasantly, dispelling fears.
When he was mounted ready to depart,
Mr. Warder said, " We are glad that you stopped,
And eased our minds. I'd like to know your name ;
So I some day the favor may return."
" My name is Lancium," the man replied.
" I am a cowboy, and live in the camps."
Now whistling, now singing to himself,
Mused Lancium as he rode upon his way,
" How strange it is to see the ladies here,
How bright and beautiful is that young girl ! "

VI.

LANCIUM.

When Lancium returned he called again
To see the friendly settlers by the way.
" I am so glad," to Mrs. Warder he said,
" To see some ladies coming to this land.
I like to be in their society.
Their presence and their voices make me think
Of my old mother and my boyhood home."

" Men never then forget however long
Away from mothers, sisters and from home,"
Mrs. Warder said, and smiled on the strong man
Who sat and mused and pulled his fine mustache.
" No, all we boys, I mean all in the camps,
Love to think o'er the years we were at home
And speculate on probabilities,
And wonder who are married, who are dead,
Of the companions of our youthful days."

Soon Lancium departed, and to camp
Made way and told his comrades the glad news,
A mutual feeling of strange pleasure came
To those lone hearts, obdurate with such life.
They felt that a new race was in the land
That would cause peace, refinement, gentleness
To be felt in the wild life at the west,
And they and all were better for the fact.

VII.

WINTER.

That fall the settlement was all astir.
The men were daily chopping in the woods;
The women worked about the lonely tents;
The children longing for discovery
Climbed knobs and hills and isolated peaks,
And looked on the arena spread beneath;
The mountains far out on the Concho
Ranged round the west until they almost met
The Brady mountains girdling the south;
And Santa Anna grand and solitary
Stood a lone wonder on the rolling plains.
The cattle grazed upon a thousand hills;
And droves of wild mustangs were here and there;
And herds of cattle, urged by the cowboys,
Were moving slowly o'er the smoky prairies,
In little droves, and ever on the watch,
The antelopes moved listlessly about.

The wolves in droves came around the camps by day
And were so beautiful they looked not fierce.
The hazy autumn atmosphere was sad,
And yellow grew the grass upon the plains.
The leaves upon the oaks grew sear, and fell,
And were blown from the woods across the plains
By the most forward blizzard of the year.
Men, women, children, worked with all their might
To make some shelter ere cold weather came.
The men worked on their buildings through the day,
And split and planed the shingles by fire-light.
In spite of all, cold weather came apace.
It was a bitter winter—such as comes
But seldom in this sunny clime of ours—
And caught the settlers unprepared for it.
In a new country, houseless and forlorn,
Blue northers stalked forth in the wintry nights,
And mercilessly swept the tents away,
And helpless children were exposed to all
The terrors of the awful wintry storm
That roared and whistled through the leafless trees,
And desolately swept the treeless hills.
They tried to light a fire, but the strong blasts
Swept it away in sparks along the ground.
Fond mothers clasped their babies to their breasts
And held them closely, to prevent the cold
From freezing the warmth out of their soft forms.
Next day, when the sun shone so brightly through
The biting air, there ever passed across
His disk bright floating threads of icy mist.

Then it would moderate, and snow would fall
And noiselessly nestle in the moldering grass.
Death stillness wrapt the sombre hills and dales.
The slowly-winding, noiseless flakes came down
In checkered flights aslant the dull, gray heights,
Till valleys, plains, and knobs and peaks and hills
Were covered o'er with soft, immaculate waves.
The smooth, black clouds would break and clear away
So suddenly, as if by magic powers;

With an unwonted brilliancy the sun
Rose, and along the limpid concave sailed.
Then lay stretched out a white and blinding sea.
The far-off hills seemed nearer, and looked like
So many promontories capped with snow,
That sparkled, trembled, twinkled in the sun
With all the tintings of the iris' hues.

VIII.

THE BUFFALO HUNT.

It was so cold the men made no headway
Upon the buildings, and they plainly saw
That they must spend the winter in the tents.
So far from market, and without money,
Provisions were alarmingly scarce.
Beyond the Colorado river, far
Away among the hills that were in view,
The buffaloes still lived in numbers vast.
Their meat was good, and free alike to all.
The settlers united, with their teams,
And went to hunt the harassed animals.
Far out among the cedar-skirted hills,
Where there ran, through rich valleys, limpid streams,
They found the mighty animals they sought.
The hunters stood upon the hills and saw,
At noon, the buffaloes come from behind
Each clump of bushes and each hill and cliff,
From all directions trailing to the streams;
From out each canyon and down slanting plains
They rushed down headlong, heedless of the claws
Of thorny cactus and speared chaparral,
That clung and clawed their rugged, woolly hides.
At midday, one by one, adown the trail
They innocently came to quench their thirst.
For several weeks the hunters slew, and stripped
The hides from off the animals, and saved
The best meat, and in boxes packed it down,

And changed the fat to lard, and put in cans.
With wagons heavy loaded, they returned,
In anxious haste, back to their families,
With a supply of meat for a long time.

The treatment of the buffalo affords
A subject melancholy in extreme—
Such as attends no other race of beasts.
A harmless animal, and good for food,
They could be tamed around the ranch like cows.
They would have been a help incalculable
Had they been left alone, except for food,
To the first settlers, when provisions were
So scarce that they could hardly be obtained.
When the Indians ceased to overrun the land,
With tomahawk and the dread scalping-knife,
Men came from east on money-making trips;
And, for the paltry sum their hides would bring,
Shot these great animals by thousands down,
And stripped the hides off, leaving the fat meat,
That would have fed for years the families
That came to make their living by hard work,
To till the soil and build the country up.
The wolf and buzzard ate their portion up.
Were these men ever smitten with remorse
When they heard the groans of these animals
As they lay dying, pierced with jagged balls?
Or, when they shot the leader down, all stopped
And watched the fallen in his agonies,
Not knowing that they stood but to be shot,
Until the last fell heavily on the ground?
Did not their senses fail them as they wrought
Destruction so unreasonable and base?
Wild animals dragged the rich flesh away,
And ever over them the buzzards flapped.
Nor did these men cease till almost extinct
Were these meek animals upon the earth:
Then slunk back to their peaceful homes again.

IX.

NIGHT ON THE PRAIRIES.

The little colony was lonely while
Most of the men were out west on the hunt.
The grown-up boys remained to do the work
About the camps, and to shield from harm and care
The women and the children in their charge.
Sometimes a stockman would ride through the camps,
Inquiring for the stock that they had lost,
And stopped to talk, relieving the dull calm.
Mrs. Warder and her children lived alone,
For Mr. Warder had gone on the hunt.
Soon as the cowboys, riding everywhere,
Passed through the settlement and learned the facts
That the women and the children were alone,
They showed them every kindness in their power.
Whene'er they killed a beef, they sent the best
Immediately to the settlers.

Across the plains one eve rode Lancium.
He kept no road, for the hills were his guides.
It was so pleasant that he aimed to camp
Out on the open plains; but as night came
A whistling blizzard blew up without clouds,
And instantly the air was freezing cold.
He looked about, but found no wood to burn,
And it was bleak and barren where he was.
He put spurs to his horse and almost flew,
Now across valley, now o'er rocky hills.
Lone Santa Anna and Bead Mountains seemed
Like animated bosom-friends to him,
So isolated in their lonely watch,
Where they had stood for ages and gazed o'er
The world of rolling plains and winding streams:
Home of mound-builders, then of savages
That chased the buffalo and swift mustang.
As Lancium travelled in the moonlit night,

And the broad prairies lay in silvery sheen,
The bleak wind swept across the treeless hills
And seemed intent on freezing him to death.
These mountains loomed up, capped with the mild
    light,
And stood as guides and pointed out his way.
He was bound for that charmed settlement
Where he hoped to find fire at Warder's camp.
Yes, there was a fire-light south of the tent,
A pile of logs aglow, fanned by the wind
That whipped around the tent and blew the sparks
About upon the ground till they went out.
He hallooed loudly when he reached the tent,
But there returned no answer; then he cried:
" May I get down and warm beside your fire?
I have been riding long across the prairie,
Facing the wind, and suffering with the cold."
A frightened voice said, " Yes, sir," from the tent.
Mrs. Warder and her children were alone,
And were scared at the man's voice in the night;
But Heclea whispered to her mother when
She heard the voice, " It is Lancium."
He knew not that the men were gone; had he,
He would not have come in the dead of night.
But when he heard no man's voice in the tent,
He told his name, and why he had been there.
Before the fire he warmed his hands and feet,
And talked with Mrs. Warder for several hours.
He learned that all the men were on the hunt,
And, in the desolation of the night,
He felt so sorry for the folks exposed.
Women, children, houseless and alone,
Must undergo such hardships in the land.
Next morning, when the family arose,
They found no man, for Lancium had gone.

X.

THE LAST BUNCH.

The winter was just verging into spring,
A bunch of buffaloes passed near the camps;
About Bead Mountain ranged they on the hills.
There were about ten head in all—old ones,
Their yearlings and young calves. They restless
    seemed,
And wandered to and fro among the stock,
On the alert, and seldom stopped to feed.
They were uneasy—knew not where to go,
They were exiles, homeless in their own land.
The children looked at them with interest,
And the men made them ready for the chase,
To shoot them down ere they could get away.
When Heclea saw her father get his gun,
She pleaded piteously for the poor things:
" O shoot them not, dear father, let them go!
They are so helpless, cut off here alone,
So far from the great herds upon the plains.
We can tell by their actions they are scared,
Bewildered, restless, know not where to flee—
Much more, they are in their old homes of yore.
How would it seem to us should we go back
To our old home, and find strange beings there
Who sought our lives and would not let us rest? "

This put it in a new light to them all,
And Mr. Warder put his gun away,
And no one chased the buffaloes that day.
They strolled among the cattle for a while,
Then passed from sight over the rolling hills.
They were the last in Coleman County seen.

BOOK II.

I.

SPRING.

UPON the western prairies the first spring
Was full of interest to the settlers.
Spring opened early, as a recompense
For the inclement winter just past o'er.
The stockmen set fire to the tall stale sedge
That everywhere grew rank upon the hills.
The ragged fires could be seen from the peaks—
A string of flame and smoke that stretched across
The prairies, and engirded many peaks;
It quietly consumed the useless grass,
The last year's surplus bounty of the plains.
The hills were transformed to a jetty black,
While the short mesquite grass that would not burn
Remained for the stock to eat in the vales.
The wind blew ever softly from the south
O'er hills, and there was ever borne about
The scent of fresh-burnt grass upon the air.
Spring showers fell upon the fire-cleansed hills;
And from the roots the tender blades sprang up
Till the green softness shone fresh in the sun,
Besprinkled with the wild flower's gaudy hues.
On the mild cloudless gala days of spring,
A band of children made Heclea their queen,
And made bold raids, and decked themselves with
        wreaths,
The regal trophies from the hills and vales.
The hollyhocks of almost every tint,
So soft and sweet, exposed to every breeze,
The daisies, bellflowers, and the lilies grew,
And vines of rattle-boxes ran about.

The cactus produced a green, smooth pear
That reddened rapidly to juicy fruit.
In ledges of the rocky cliffs there grew
The thorny bushes called the chaparral,
O'erburdened with plump berries, clear and red—
A fruit delicious as of any land.
Each berry was protected by speared leaves
That pricked the hand that tried to pluck the fruit;
But when the fruit was ripe, ready to drop,
The gatherers spread clean sheets around the stems,
And shook the bushes till the berries lay
In piles, with dry twigs and leaves, on the sheets.

Strange things, the children ne'er had seen before,
Aroused unbounded interest in them.
The baby prairie-dogs played on the mounds,
Or, frightened, barking, ran into the holes;
The mule-eared rabbits crouched in the tall sedge,
And, when a person suddenly approached,
They bounded up—with ears back, sped away.
One day the children watched, with saddened hearts,
A mule-eared rabbit chased by a coyote.
The wolf and rabbit both were nearly spent.
The rabbit laid his ears upon his back—
The way they always do when closely pressed;
The wolf, with lolling tongue, pursued its prey,
Until both disappeared over the hill.
The children wished that they could have helped the
        hare,
And never knew whether it escaped or not.
Calves numberless upon the prairies were,
That played about their mothers as they grazed
Or, bleating, ran to meet the lowing cows;
Or lay as dead when hidden in the grass,
While the mothers went to the creek to drink;
And naught could rouse them from their lethargy
Except the soft, low moo, which, when they heard,
They jumped up wildly and ran to the cows;
And many little antelopes were seen,
That, bounding nimbly, kept up with the flock.

Both old and young, as they traversed dog-towns,
Looked anxiously about them as they went;
A dreaded enemy lurked round the holes—
The rattlesnake, that warns before it strikes.
Sometimes the rattlers sang down in the holes,
Or lay, their scaly bodies spiral-formed,
The rattles turned up trembling in the air;
And, on the beautifully-rounded coil,
The head lay in the attitude to strike.
All things inhabiting the western prairie
Lived in continual dread of these vile pests,
And jumped and ran as from no other sound
Whene'er they heard that ill-portending buzz—
The warning that must quickly be obeyed.
And ugly little owls lived in the holes—
The only things that cared not for the snakes.

And o'er the plains the Western Texas skies
Arched o'er and met the glories of the hills;
The azure deepened to a deeper hue
Where'er it mingled with the haze of hills.
White flecks of clouds sailed o'er the azure vault;
Their shadows, falling, glided o'er the hills,
And traversed verdant plains, and rested on
The sides of peaks, and could be seen for miles.
And rain could be seen far upon the plains;
Blown by the wind, the water fell in curves—
A dusky sheet connecting clouds to earth—
And hid the hills, and plains, and trees beyond,
And looked like rising mist on the hillsides.

II.

THE FIRST TEMPLES.

When grass, and flowers, and leaves, and balmy
    winds,
And spring-time glorious, multitudinous
In natural grandeur, reigned upon the plains,

Before they built a shelter for themselves,
The settlers made rude arbors of the oaks,
And met beneath them, where they worshipped God.
The little beams crept through the brush, and made
Bright spots upon the children's golden curls,
And played about the cheeks of maidens fair,
And were the only jewels that they wore.
The settlers next built houses for their schools,
Low, and of unhewn logs—the floor was dirt;
The roof above them was made of the same;
The cracks were stopped with mortar made of mud.
The children were sent to school through the fall
And winter, and worked the rest of the year.

III.

THE COWBOYS.

In cow-camps and among the settlements
Were many boys that breathed the bracing air,
And exercised both brains and limbs at work:
In plowing oxen, breaking the tough sod;
Or riding madly o'er the rocks and streams;
Or roping, throwing, branding horses and cows.
These boys grew up to manhood's noblest cast
In Freedom's lap—the boundless prairies.   They
Knew only freedom, and looked upon all
Upon the earth as equal, rich or poor.
Nor laws, nor prison bars can ever take,
Without their lives, this heaven-born gift of theirs.

No hungry man e'er passed by a cow-camp;
For people of all ages, colors, climes,
That came prospecting, or passed through the West,
Were hospitably received by the cowboys.
They treated rich and poor exactly alike;
The cattle king and landlord were the same
To them as the tramp, plodding with his stick.
Sometimes, like all, they liked to have some fun,
And they could tell a tenderfoot on sight.

Those who lived in the camps, with only men,
Thought women spotless angels on the earth—
Some superhuman beings, wondrous fair.
If one, while riding round, came on a camp
Of emigrants, and there were ladies there,
He told his comrades, and each one found some
Excuse—went to inquire about their stock,
And hoped that way to get a glimpse of them
And those who lived within the pale of home,
A mother's influence surrounding them ;
And in a sister's sweet society,
Where there were no temptations thrown about
Of social life, to lure them on to sin ;
And then there were the blessed faces of
The matchless Christian mothers of the West,
With wondrous patience and with tender care
They watched over their children as they grew,
In isolated ways, amid the wilds,
Evincing an untiring fortitude
That casts the Spartan mothers in the shade.
These boys could hardly stay away from home,
And, when out working after cattle, were
So glad when they were on their homeward way-
Those great big boys who loved their mothers so,
They held all women sacred for her sake ;
And would have given their lives in the defence
Of any woman, however much depraved.

IV.

THE ROUND-UP.

Now Lancium was the youngest in the camp;
The cowboys called him, "Lady of the Ranch,"
Because of ways and form effeminate,
Although he had turned out a fine mustache,
And had just passed his twenty-second year.
He had been for three years in the same camp.
He was quiet, modest, never joining in

The obscene stories told around the fire;
But, stranger still, no one e'er heard him swear.
Such virtues in so wild and rough a place
Soon drew attention and respect from all.
Thus he was the beloved favorite
Of boss and all the cowboys in the camp.
When spring came and the flowers bedecked the
      plains,
And the fresh grass became luxuriant,
The cattle that grazed on it all the day
Dropped the old hair and became sleek and fat.

Then they were gathered to take on the trail.
From the surrounding country all were brought
Into a herd upon a level plain
Where was found the fewest of the hidden holes
Of the small prairie dogs, where the horse steps,
Turns somerset, and dashes the cowboy
With lightning speed into eternity;
Or rolling o'er him, crushes in his ribs.
In one vast herd the lowing cows and steers
Were driven from the land where they were raised
On the long weary trail toward the North.

The children of the settlement ran out
With eagerness to watch the herd pass by,
And see the cowboys dash around the rear.
Two cowboys always rode before a herd,
To drive the cattle of the range out of
The path, lest they should get into the herd,
And be, unnoticed, driven from their range;
These cowboys drove the milk-cows to the woods.
They heard the cattle low, the cowboys' whoop;
The leading steers came running round the hill,
For it was warm and dry, they had come far
Since they left the last water, and they sniffed
The moisture of the stream that was before.
Two cowboys rode up to the Warders' tent,
And asked if they could get a drink of water.
One of these cowboys, equipped for the trail,

Was Lancium, whom the family recognized
With courtesies, and, smiling, Heclea
Gave them the water with her dimpled hands.
Her cheeks were soft as the wildflowers around.
" Where are you driving to ? " Mrs. Warder asked.
" To Kansas," Lancium slowly replied.
" When may we look for you back here ? " she
    asked.
" Next fall, if nothing happens," he replied.
" I hope you will, and sometimes call on us,
We have come to look on you as our own."
A softening feeling mastered Lancium
That he had not experienced for long years,
And he replied, " Thank you, I hope so too."

Then Lancium and his partner rode away.
" What friends you have made here ! " his comrade
    said.
" You are so lucky, would that I were so !
What a fine woman that young girl will make !
While she is young you will have a good chance
To win her love, while it is hers to give ;
For when she reaches perfect womanhood
All the cowboys will fight to win the prize ;
But you will be sole owner of her heart.
Her cheeks remind me of the hollyhocks,
So various tinted is their changing glow."

Then a new hope was born to Lancium
That was so sweet in his lone cowboy's life ;
And from the light comparison he loved
The wild-flowers that the cattle trod upon,
And felt that when his horse passed over them
That he was bruising the soft feelings of
The fair sweet girl that he had come to know.

In couples all the cowboys came to drink,
And Heclea, smiling sweetly, handed them
The water while they watched her dimpled hands,
And caught a glimpse of her fresh, girlish face—

Almost hid by her bonnet closely drawn
Around her soft white brow and shining curls.
The cowboys did not come for water, but
To get a glimpse of the fair ladies there
Whom Lancium had told them of so much.

V.

THE TRAIL.

Proceeded Lancium on the weary trail
Through almost sleepless nights and toilsome days.
When the cattle became broken to the road,
They patiently moved on their fateful way,
As if resigned to their sad destiny

For weeks the herd moved slowly toward the North
For the beeves had to graze along the way.
The cowboys rounded-in the herd at night,
And every one stood guard part of the night,
Proceeding from, or coming to the camp,
Or riding to and fro upon his beat—
For each one rode around the herd until
He met his comrade, then turned back and rode
Backward and forward over the same space,
So that no beef could stray off from the herd.
He whistled, sang, or shouted as he rode
So that the cattle would know what he was,
For so much like we humans in a land
Where everything is strange, they timid were,
And took fright at strange objects in the dark.
If anything came prowling round the herd
With outlines ghostly in the shades of night,
They broke in panic, and, ungovernable,
Dashed wildly, madly, carrying everything,
And trampling under foot all in their path.
And the cowboys pursued the clattering herd,
And dashed around them on their trained steeds,
Which never were so faithful as at night—

While trying to retain the frightened beasts,
And hallooed soothingly until the beeves
Were quieted.   Sometimes the beeves were scattered
In the stampede, and wandered aimlessly
O'er hills and streams and prairies strange to them,
Till all were killed by Indians in their glee.
The cowboys as they mounted every hill,
With hands over their eyes, scanned anxiously
The valleys, streams, and woods that lay beneath,
To see if any Indians lurked about.
And many other trail-herds were in sight
Long lines of cattle, all bound the same way.
Sometimes the boys, so long without repose,
Dozed and fell from their saddles on the way.
Unshaved and dirty they rode through the heat,
And toiled on patiently through dust and rain
And rode around the herd on stormy nights,
On the bare prairies where no shelter was.
The wind unchecked swept over the bare plains
And dashed the rain and hail against their cheeks,
While o'er them in the jetty vault above
The lightning spread out in wan lurid sheets
Or pierced with forked tongues the black concave,
And, crashing, rolling, and reverberating
The thunder o'er them held high carnival.

One night in the wild Indian Territory,
While Lancium was stationed on relief,
A thunder-storm broke on them in its might.
The lightning played about his horse's mane,
And through its glare the glistening rain poured
     down,
Through which he saw the cattle standing still.
Their bodies looked strange, shadowy, beyond
A sheeny mist unnatural in its make.
They seemed so much more patient than he was,
His heart went out to them, and the tears rose
Into his eyes, and mingled with the rain.
They knew not that they were on their last drive,
And stood without complaint in a strange land,

Driven from their own range never to return.
The cowboys might return to their own homes,
And many happy days yet to enjoy,
While these poor brutes in a few days must die
To satisfy the hunger of the world,
And after death forgotten evermore.

VI.

THE SETTLEMENT.

Again return we to the settlement.
The fertile valleys were fenced round about,
And patient oxen broke the matted sod,
And, uncomplaining, up and down the row
They drew the plow from morning until night,
Nor seemed to grow impatient of the task,
As acre after acre was upturned.

The little herds became located and
Ranged ever close around their new-made homes.
It was something pathetic how they liked
To be near the familiar people who
Had brought them to this land of grass and stream.
The colts came homeward as at measured times
And wistfully looked over in the yard,
And watched the children at their thoughtless play.
Whene'er the twilight stole across the plains
There always rose a rattling of hoofs.
Great brawny steers seemed never at their ease
Until they had lain down about the pens,
And then, with air contented, chewed their cuds,
Or threw their heads round to their sides and slept.
The milk-cows always led this homeward march
And, lowing restlessly, stood round the pen
And watched their calves until they were turned in,
And stood so patiently to be milked while
They were where they could lick their chubby calves.

Methinks those quiet mild-eyed animals
Did more good while provisions were so scarce
To the first settlers on the wild frontier,
Than rangers, soldiers, or the Alamo.

VII.

THE TELEGRAPH LINE.

When they first pitched their tents on western
  lands,
The only thing that met the movers' view,
Constructed as they knew by human hands,
Was the new governmental telegraph
That ran from Fort Worth to Fort Concho.

This line was built by convict suffering.
These poor men had to work ten hours each day,
While cruel masters stood round with the lash,
And many times unmercifully beat
Them while chained down upon the lonely plains;
And there was no power to redress their wrongs.
At night they were chained to the wagon-wheels,
With heavy shackles on their wrists and legs.
The cowboys and the settlers were glad
When those men went away; their cruel ways
Were an abomination in the land.

The settlers felt that this lone human work
Across the wilds was company to them.
Now rising, sinking, across hills and vales,
Receding through the glistening mirages,
And lost to view as it ran over hills,
Where in the distance ever seems to rest
A semi-melancholy azure haze,
That gives such dreamlike scenery to the West.

The children put their ears to the posts,
And listened to what they supposed the news

Of the great world, which hummed as it passed by,
While it was but the buzzing of the wind
That played upon the wire which ran across
The broad and open prairies of the West.

VIII.

ARMS.

All men went fully armed. There was no law
Preventing it, because men felt their need
As they were riding o'er the lonely land.
E'en ministers of the Gospel as they went
Across the prairies to their meeting-places,
Wore belts of cartridges clasped round their waists,
And large revolvers hanging at their sides.

On the broad prairies, once upon a time,
Two ministers met—on the roadless wilds—
That had not met before for fifteen years,
And grasped each other's hands in glad surprise.

The rangers came around; the settlers felt
Secure from danger while they were about.
Many negro soldiers passed along the road,
Bound for Fort Concho. Their uniform
Of blue and buttons shone bright in the sun.

IX.

1878.

The year eighteen hundred and seventy-eight
Was one of great depression in the West,
For finances were dead throughout the land;
And many footmen passed along the road,
Proceeding to the governmental posts

In quest of work.   They asked food on the way.
Worn, weary, without money, many came
To Warder's house, and asked for food to eat.
Bread was a scarcity, meat plentiful,
Still the settlers never turned those men away,
Though most of them were foreigners, and could
Not speak distinctly.   Heclea loved to wait
On those tired, homeless men.   It was, she felt,
One little chance to do good; for she longed
To be of some use, some good in the world,
To mix with it and be felt for her good;
And it would know that she was part of it.

X.

A CONFESSION.

One day a man called at the house, who had
Known Mr. Warder when they both were boys.
He heard the name called somewhere, and was glad,
As was the way upon the wild frontier,
To even hear the name of an old friend.
He hastened to the place where Warder lived.

They talked of their past lives since last they met.
But there was sadness in the visitor's tale:
Oppression had made him a desperate man,
But he made bare his life to his old friend,
And Heclea gazed with pity on the man
While listening to the hardships he had borne.
Addressing all, with silence, thus he spoke:

" Before I came to this free western land
I had become a man of the worst type.
I had killed several men; was forced to flee
To some place where the law could reach me not.
One consolation I have—that is peace.
Those men were cruel tyrants that I slew;
They harassed me, my friends, and those I loved

Beyond endurance.   I could take no more.
I had heard in the state where I was raised
That none but cut-throats could exist out here;
That theft and murder held untrammeled sway
That all the outlawed rakes of other states
Found an asylum here safe from the law.
I came here, and I found all was not true
That I had read in papers of the North.
True, many came here to escape the law.
Though not a thief, I saw the thief found out,
The doors were open to him everywhere,
And all were glad to give of what they had;
He grew ashamed, and then forbore to steal.

" I came here mainly to escape the law.
I looked about me, and all was in peace.
No one suspected me, all seemed so glad
That I had come to make my home with them.
No one to censure me or dog my path.
I was so much alone, and often when
Out travelling, long without the sight of man,
There crept o'er me a sad, strange loneliness,
And I wooed the good-will of all I met.
It is the greatest pleasure now I know
E'en to behold a gracious woman's face.
No, this land makes good men and citizens
Of criminals and outcasts of other states.
A ranger now I am, and trusted much,
And honored for my bravery everywhere,
Commissioned to protect the settlements.
No vestige of my old life now remains;
I would not, could not, now commit a crime."

XI.

PLUM GATHERING.

The sultry days of August had passed by;
A hazy atmosphere hung o'er the land,

Imparting a sad aspect to the hills,
And seemed to almost form a thick blue mist
Along the winding streams, seen from the hills.
The grass had turned from green to reddish brown;
The mesquite trees were overcharged with beans,
That hung in clusters, rattling with the breeze.
Abundance of wild plums grew on the creeks;
The bushes chose in rocky cliffs to grow,
And interlaced their limbs with thorny clasps.
At this time they were full of soft red plums.
Though sour, to the settlers they were good.
Their orchards were not old enough to bear.
The plums were all the fruit in the new land
That ripened in this season of the year

When Indian summer saddened all the land,
One morning, while the air was cool and fresh
For the walk, Heclea and the children went
To gather plums all day upon Home creek.
The children cried out with delight, as they
Came unexpectedly on a new prize.
They worked oblivious of all else besides.
So eagerly they picked the plump red fruit,
They noticed not that it was clouding up,
Till, suddenly, a thunder-clap crashed in,
That shook the earth and echoed down the creek.
The sun shone brightly, for not yet o'ercast
Was half the heavens by the thick black cloud;
It was a rain-storm gathering overhead—
A characteristic of the western clime.
The children, frightened, came round Heclea
As the loud thunder rolled about o'erhead.
She felt a sad responsibility,
A melancholy loneliness and fear,
To try the frightened children to compose.
She knew that they must take the wind and rain;
Yet felt that the storm would not injure them—
The children, so defenceless and alone.
Some horsemen were then riding down the creek,
And Heclea beheld them and exclaimed;

7

" See, children, several men are riding there!
If they would stop we would not be so lonely."

The children watched them wistfully, then cried:

" They see us, they are coming straight this way ! "
There came a puff of wind just then, the rain
Began to spatter, and the thunder pealed.

" Why, children, are you out here in the rain ? "
Asked one of them, as they came dashing up.
He spoke so kindly, Heclea looked at him,
And Lancium she quickly recognized.
Immediately her fears vanished away ;
She felt at ease in sweet security.
He recognized her simultaneously.

" Why, is it you, Miss Heclea ? " he asked,
And bowed and raised his hat, and she began :

" We came to gather plums, and noticed not
That clouds were gathering till the thunder pealed."

" You and your mother let me warm before
Your fire upon that awful bitter night—
Do you remember it ? I always shall.
Now I the favor will return ; I'm glad
That I have the occasion so to do."

The cowboys took their saddles off, untied
The slickers from behind the saddles, and
One told the children to stand side by side.
One slicker, two or three of them reached round,
Protecting them as one of the cowboys.
But Lancium kindly held his slicker up,
While Heclea put her arms into the sleeves ;
He buttoned it down to her feet.   Then took
His broad-brimmed hat, and said : " Miss Heclea,
You will get wet with that thin bonnet on ;
Will you wear my hat ? "

But she archly asked:

" What will you do yourself ? "

" Oh, I can do

'Most any way," he lightly made reply.

The rain in chilling drifts fell for a while.
In spite of the great broad-brimmed hat, the wind
Blew sprays of water against Heclea's cheeks,
And soaked her straying ringlets till they clung
Like love vines coiling on her snow-white brow.

Meanwhile, talked Lancium with unfeigned delight;
For he was happy, but he knew not why.
He looked so gallant as he nobly strove
To interest the fair girl at his side.
He told her of the dusky squaws he saw
While passing through the Indian Territory,
And many wild adventures on the trail,
Until the shower had passed.   The children were
Ashamed that they had been so frightened at
A thing which brought so much good to the earth.
The grass and flowers in moistened softness glowed ;
The trees took on a brighter, fresher tint,
And purer, softer blew the gentle breeze.

BOOK III.

I.

HECLEA.

FAIR Heclea ripened into womanhood
Environed with the prairies and the hills,
And all that could enchant a heroine's life
Amid the glamour of romantic wilds.
It made no difference, and all was good,
If the sunbeams that spanned the universe
Should kiss the fairest thing they found too roughly :
Or the breezes that ever lived in ceaseless motion,
And swept across the prairies unopposed,
Should strike against her tender cheeks too hard :
She lived a peerless being in the wilds—
Was held as more than human by rough men.
Her eyes grew soft and liquid as she saw
The wild-flowers deck the plains in gaudy hues,
Arrayed by the soft fingers of the spring,
The bright, warm sunbeams vivifying all.

And something of the West—its sunny clime,
Its matchless skies stretched o'er its tinted plains,
Its boundless prairies and its heavenly air,
Its freedom unconstrained, its easy ways,
Its dreamy sheen—seemed in the make of her.
Her eyes partook the azure of its skies,
And from their depths the hallowed light of love
Lit up the sweet expression of her face.

A peace ineffable was round her life,
A charm entrancing in her words and ways,
As when at night, upon the summer plains,

The moon, serene and quiet, queenly moves
Across the stage uncurtained o'er the plains ;
And the enraptured traveller watches her
Sweep by the glowing planets in her course,
And, passing, pales the chained galaxy,
And all the hills and peaks are silver-gilt
By the mild light reflected from her train.
The prairie-dogs are sleeping in their holes;
The coyotes fear to wander forth and howl
When there is such pure light upon the plains.
There are no woods, the haunt of whip-poor-wills
Or screech-owls, startling him with mournful cries.
There is no sound but the soft whisperings
Of love of the caressing breezes, as
They bid him lie upon the downy grass,
And they will cool his forehead while he sleeps.

The cloudless, vernal sun, that shed his light
In all directions on the western plains,
Enlivening, vivifying everything,
Was seen in the expression of her face,
As she looked kindly on all that she saw.
That face, so pleasing, fair, and beautiful,
Was worshipped by the rough men who had lived
For many years upon the wild frontier
Without once seeing a sweet, lovely girl,
Or hearing the soft music of her voice.

II.

LOVE.

Came Lancium often to see Heclea,
And she grew lovelier each day ; new charms
Became her property : a graceful bearing;
A dignified expression of the face ;
A modest light of womanish pride beamed
From her eyes, different from that of the girl :
The charm of the true woman, her great power—

A proud yet lovable complaisance—
Was round about her in its purity.
And in the spring and summer Lancium came,
And went with her to meeting, where were held
The services beneath the arbor's shade,
Or in the low-roofed houses, made of logs,
Where met they when the weather was severe.

Meek Heclea idolized this handsome man,
And watched his coming with a throbbing heart,
With glowing eyes, and cheeks suffused with red;
And far across the prairie, as he came,
With outline bedimmed by the trembling sheen,
She recognized him by his riding air,
And gladly watched the object she so loved
Grow more familiar as he neared her;
And side by side they rode o'er hills and vales,
And drank the strength of the flower-laden breezes.

When away from her, Lancium thought of Heclea
Continually, and how blank was his life
Ere his love for her made it beautiful!
How changed he had seemed since he had known
    her!
And, miles away, when riding on the lines,
He would oft check his horse on a hill-top,
And gaze at the blue hills around her home.
How dear and beautiful they seemed to him,
Because they brought fond memories of her!
The keenest sorrow that he knew were fears
That she might go away—might wed
Some one ere he could tell her of his love;
But she was young, and that was hope to him.
If she were taken far away, what would
Life be to him?   The western land
Would be a beautiful and lonely wild,
Devoid of everything of love and life.
But a sweet intuition had oft told
Him he was not indifferent to her.
Perhaps it came to him as oft to men—

A deep, unguarded love-look of the eyes,
That speaks a language that is known to all
A gentle tone of voice she used for him,
An easy resignation in his presence;
And this strange intimation of her love
Was the keenest joy he had ever **known.**

III.

THE PET ANTELOPE.

One day in spring brought Lancium a gift
To his beloved Heclea to give.
A little antelope he had picked up
Upon the prairie where it lay alone.
He knew that the cute thing would please her much,
And graciously presented it to her.

She thanked him kindly, for the thought of her,
And prized it much, because a gift from him.

On milk she fed it, it grew plump and gay;
It went to the pen where they milked the cows,
And drank the fresh warm milk out of a pail.
It was a lovely pet, and gamboled much;
Where'er the children went, it followed them.
It liked for Heclea to fondle it;
And often Lancium, in wonder, sat
And watched her soft white hands rest on its head,
Or smooth the mossy hair upon its back.

When it was grown and was so dear to her,
One day, in summer, as the boys rode
The horses to the creek, a mile away,
It followed them, as was its wont.
It stopped half way to graze till they returned.
A cowboy came riding across the prairie,
And drew near to it, for it knew no fear,
And, thinking it a wild one, shot it down.

IV.

THE MOUNDS.

One evening, Lancium called on Heclea,
And they rode out together o'er the hills.
They climbed to the top of a lofty peak
Where grew small cedars clumped among the rocks,
And hackberries grew and clung o'er the pits,
The violated Indian graves, where men,
In search of treasures, dug the red bones up.

They rode along Home creek, and checked their
    steeds,
And paused a moment to survey the mounds
That, in large numbers, are along that stream.
These mounds are seen in all parts of the West.
They are always upon the banks of streams,
In bends embowered with the mighty trees,
And near clear living water. They are round,
And form a basin filled with black burnt dirt,
That lapse of ages has washed down and sunk
From the debris of rocks and coal around.
The rock that enters in these mounds is charred
And blackened as if burnt almost to lime.
These mounds were built by man, there is no doubt:
Their make-up bears the impress of his hands;
Their symmetry the planning of his mind.

Now, all over the West, there still remain
The footprints of a vanished race of men,
Lone ruins that of a lost people tell,
As those of Babylon and Nineveh.

Who were these people? And from whence came
    they?
How did they live? And whither did they go?

They are a people buried in mystery:
Their history, their ways of life, their looks
Are lost, and will be lost forevermore.

V.

A WESTERN SUNSET.

As Lancium and Heclea rode home,
The sun hung just above the western hills;
The eve was pleasant as the day was warm,
For a cool breeze was blowing from the south,
That stealthily and noiselessly stole by.
And as they rode down in the small ravines
The warm air struck them, but soon passed away
As they mounted the breeze-loved rolling hills.

The sun shone with a bright though less fierce
    glare
Than in the morning.   As he sank adown
The limpid atmosphere along the west,
A lovely mildness seemed within his rays.
He sank behind a black and jagged peak,
That was sublimely margined with the gold ,
And the last lingering rays just kissed the hills,
And seemed reluctant to withdraw and leave
The world in darkness.   Then, ecliptic-like,
They shot athwart the rapidly darkening skies,
And shone across the heavens in light and shade

" How sad and lonely it is to be out
Upon the prairie, after the sun is set.
It makes me feel a greater reverence
For the diviner Power," said Heclea.

" I have camped out so much," said Lancium,
" I like the twilight on the prairie.   It seems
To draw around the earth its mantle,
And shuts from view the broad expanse of space
And drives away the glaring light of day."

The sun is gone, and all the stars come out,
And Venus sparkles with unwonted light ;
And just below her is thrown up the sun's
Last lingering flood of light, resembling
A mighty geyser of bright liquid gold.

VI.

AUTUMN.

The autumn on the western prairies was
At that time sad, weird, fanciful and grand.
The Indian summer skies hung o'er the hills,
And looked as if one could reach out his hand
And scrape the dusky film, it seemed so near.
To a man travelling alone there came
A longing for a home and company.

Now, times have changed. The autumn still re-
        turns,
The smutty haze still settles round the hills,
And soft winds sway the yellow brittle sedge ;
But that constrained loneliness is gone :
Fine houses sit in grandeur on the hills,
'Mid live oaks. Fences made of wire are stretched
Around the valleys, on the flowing streams.
And, in the autumn, cribs and granaries
Are filled to overflowing. Stacks of hay
Are steepling each hill. The sorghum stands
In shocks in the fields. The people want
For nothing, and music and mirth is theirs.
The erstwhile prospect desolate is gone.

One eve in autumn Lancium rode across
The prairie, musing sadly, though he knew
Not why he should. Strange longings his heart,
Things on his mind that ne'er were there before.
An aspect as of twilight wrapt the world,
And the same twilight seemed around his soul ;
The stealthy winds, as they blew through the sedge
That looked like waves, made a low, mournful sound ;
The live-oaks, that in winter are so bright
In verdure evergreen, upon the hills
Showed only their dark outlines through the haze.

His thoughts were resting on fair Heclea.
O how sweet it would be to be with her,

And be always with her, in a quiet home!
The general sadness of the autumn world
Made the sweet image even more sublime.
He knew that she must feel sad and alone
As she looked out upon the gloomy plains.
Those soft blue eyes, that always seemed to him
As if created never to look on
Aught of sin, sadness, or of grief, or death,
Or anything deformed, dark, vicious, fell.
He feared their clear and beauteous depths would be
Marred by the harsh world they must look upon.

He came in sight of her home, and it seemed
The sweetest, dearest spot on earth just then;
For he felt she was there, and still unchanged
By his sad musings or the sombre day—
A gracious face and sunny, golden curls,
That was the sweetest thing on earth to him.
Forsaken, sad he felt, but brighter grew
The prescient hope of something better yet—
A home with her in their own western land.
The boundless prairies would be like his love;
The cloudless skies, vaulting o'er tinted hills,
Would smile in summer beauty over them;
And night, which is so grand upon the plains,
Would hold the galaxy as if to drop
It as a jewelled crown around their lives
If she could love him. Could that ever be?
If she should love him, what would troubles be—
The piercing blizzard, or the drifting rain,
That falls on the cowboy's unsheltered head.

VII.

THE DRIFT.

In Western Texas, generally but one
Snow falls in the same winter; for it is
So mild that the snow soon melts off.

In eighteen hundred and eighty winter broke
Quite early, with a snow that slowly fell
For several hours, and covered up the grass.
A whistling, piercing, freezing blizzard came
Upon its rear and glazed it o'er with ice;
And for ten days, although the sun shone out,
The icy wind protected the cement,
As it swept o'er the clear and glistening hills,
So it broke not to bare the grass for food.
The shivering, starving stock forlornly turned
Their heads and drifted wildly toward the south.

To the Brady Mountains the cowboys had come
From all the ranches to hold the stock back;
For only a few passes broke this chain,
And, if the cattle should once pass this range,
Would never be got back. With several boys,
Lancium was stationed to guard one pass.

They stood upon the Brady peaks, and saw
A sight as grand as ever mortal saw.
A broad arena lay upon the north,
Through which the Colorado river ran,
And numberless small streams—its tributaries;
The Concho mountains stretched around the west,
And Antelope Knob range lay on the north;
Santa Anna and Bead Mountains stood alone.

When the cowboys first turned their eyes upon
This basin it was a white, blinding flash,
As when one suddenly looks at the sun;
But when their eyes got used to the fierce glare,
They saw it was alive with drifting stock.
The dusky, moving, serpentine-like strings
Rushed southward o'er the rolling main of snow,
And nothing could have looked more desolate.
Heart-rending was the scene! Maddened with the
    cold
And gnawing hunger, they knew not what to do.
The cruel wind blew their hair the wrong way;

With bodies numb and drawn, and drooping limbs,
With heads down, shivering, and with half-closed
    eyes,
With instinct turned they toward the sunny south.
Many grew weak from want of food, sank down,
And the stiff carcasses made a brown spot
Upon the snow, feast for the greedy wolves.
The craunching, screaking of ten thousand hoofs,
That cut out blood-stained paths through frozen
    snow,
The forlorn lowing of ten thousand throats,
Were borne by whistling winds o'er treeless plains,
A mingling of melancholy wails
Accompanying the sight of bleak, cold hills.

  The cowboys, with sheer recklessness, spurred on
Their trained horses o'er the glazed rocks,
And down the glassy slopes headlong they plunged,
Without a thought of safety, life, or limbs.
The ponies strove heroically to keep
Their feet while turning back the maddened steers.
The cattle seemed deaf to the cowboys' cries;
As one was forced back, facing the raw wind,
Another rushed in, filling up the breach.

  And Lancium, heedless of life or limbs,
Spurred his horse down a steep declivity;
The feet slipped from the noble animal,
And, quick as flash of light upon the snow,
He fell, with heavy force, upon the ice;
And Lancium's brow struck, with sickening thud,
Upon the matted ice, and snow, and rocks;
And there closed over him a silent sea
Of dark oblivion; and Heclea,
Love, longings, fears, the hopes of life, stern toil,
Were blotted out by midnight blackness, and
Cold nothingness spread his quiet reign o'er him.

VIII.

THE AWAKENING.

When Lancium came to, he looked around.
He was in a small room, and curtains drawn
Shut out the light. His mind was blank, and all
Around was strange. Two cowboys sat near by.
He heard the forlorn wind wail round the house,
And the bleak, chilling aspirations caused
A shivering tremor to pass through his frame.
One of the men that sat near by the bed
Rose, and, crossing the room, slowly drew back
One of the curtains from the small window,
And Lancium saw he was one of his pards.
Immediately he spoke to him, and asked
Him where he was, and what had taken place.
He learned it all. His horse had fallen down;
He had received an awful shock, and they
Bore him, unconscious, to the nearest house,
Where lived a man and wife on a cow-camp.

In a few days the wind lulled, and the snow
Melted away, and mild weather set in.
One evening Lancium was strolling round
The pens—he had not ridden since his fall—
When a lone horseman came riding to him.
He looked familiar, and, as he drew near,
Lancium recognized Mr. Warder's oldest son.
O how he loved him as he greeted him,
Because his features looked like Heclea's!

" We heard that you were sick," the boy said,
" And I came to see how you were getting on.".

A flush spread over Lancium's face.
Did Heclea think of him while he was sick?
He wished he knew, but he dared not to ask.
" I am all right now; I was not hurt much."
And Lancium took the boy to the house
And cared for him until he returned home.

BOOK IV.

I.

"I HAVE NEVER LOVED BUT YOU, LANCIUM."

SPRING had come; with it, bright skies, singing
    birds,
And plains of soft, green grass, and balmy winds,
Ere Lancium came back to Heclea;
And it seemed ages since he had seen her.
And from the wintry toil and exposure
He came to her as to his heavenly home;
For her heart opened to him in its love,
As precious as the golden gates ajar.

She met him with a sweet but half-sad smile
And an unwonted softness of the face.
Her golden tresses fell loose round her neck,
And ringlets played about her brow and cheeks;
Her fresh young face was lit with love; she was
A true personification of the spring.

They strolled forth, arm-in-arm. The morn was
    fair,
And everything seemed glad with love to them;
And neither spoke for long. Then Lancium
Said, with voice tremulous, his breath came fast:

"I cannot stand it longer, Heclea,
To live without telling you of my love;

And, if it be without avail, it will
Be a great, great ease to my tired heart
If you but listen patiently to me.
You would not coldly reject any one,
I know.   But if you feel no love for me,
I blame you not; for it will be my lot
To suffer.   Reject me without reserve.
Since I first saw you that day at the camp
I have loved you—loved you with all my heart;
And my love has increased in strength each time
That I have seen you since ;—new charms I saw
As you became the woman you now are.
It has been the prime joy I have known.
In loving you I loved all things besides ;
And it makes me so happy that I loved
A woman so much worthy of such love.
This love is pure, though from a source unworthy ;
All persons, and all things surrounding you,
Or put you in my mind, I loved so well.
I loved my very heart for loving you.
I never loved before ; no words of love
Have I e'er spoken to a girl before."

"I have never loved but you, Lancium.
I loved you when I first saw you that day
You came to our camp.   And never did
A woman more supremely love a man.
When every one was lonely here because
The country was so sparsely settled, I
Was satisfied, because that you were here.
I would not have exchanged my home for wealth
In any land if you could not be there.
And, when I heard that you were injured, I feared
That you might die, and endured days and nights
Of anguish in continued thoughts of you ;
And, do you know that I at last persuaded
My brother to go and see how you were ?
Yes, I have ever loved you, Lancium,
And it delights me to know you love me."

II.

A NEW ORDER OF THINGS.

About this time things underwent a change:
A stock country was transformed into one
Of agriculture; and a westward rush
Of emigration raised the price of land;
And every scheme was worked to dispossess
The pioneer settlers of their homes.
Up to this time the people had been free;
The rich and poor were on equality,
And every word denoting servitude
Was as an abhorred term of some dead tongue.
But from Europe came a scum, called lords,
And bought some land, and superciliously
Tried to draw a line 'tween the rich and poor.
With innocent depravity marvelous,
They would not speak to, or ask into their houses,
The most free-hearted people of the earth,
But for whose goodness they could not have lived—
No friendly hand-shake and no genial smile,
And every one was treated as a thief.

III.

LO!

The settlers whose history we have touched
When they stopped on the land which they improved,
Knew it was school land, and the property
Of a neighboring county. And this county had
An agent living in the town near them.
The settlers went to him; he made fair promises,
And showed them notes from the commissioners
Of the county which owned these lands, which **gave**
Him full power to treat with settlers.
They might go on it in full confidence

That they would find a home there, and could pay
For the lands year by year at easy rates;
But year by year no contracts made with them.
The land was not upon the market yet;
The county needed not the funds, and would
Wait till the settlers had put in their farms
And made enough on the land to pay for it.
But in that county new officers were chosen,
And they kept not their predecessors' words,
But invested a new agent with power
To sell the lands at once. The settlers should
Have a chance to buy their homes, if they would
Pay the cash down, and at the agent's price.
They knew the settlers could not meet these terms,
And the commissioners had contracted
Already to sell it all in a mass
To a land sharper and a soulless wretch,
Who would make no terms with the settlers,
Except that they must pay him the cash down.

And, lo! when, after many years had passed,
The settlers had put in extensive farms;
Their orchards had begun to bear them fruit,
And they had come to love their homes so well—
Their children ne'er had known another place—
This tyrant came along, with might empowered,
And claimed the lands that they had settled on;
And told them they must pay him then and there,
And asked exorbitant prices for the lands.

The women and the children stood in groups,
And, with pale faces and with sighs of fear,
They watched the demon's agent as he came
And called the men out to show them his deeds.
The farmers offered him their little herds
If he would only let them live in peace.
The monster said he would take nothing but
The cash. The settlers could not get the cash.
So this man went and brought the sheriff out,
And posted notices upon the walls

Of their own houses,—If they did not pay
The cash, they must leave by a certain time,
And could take nothing with them but their crops.

And thus they left their homes, and settled 'new.
The houses went to wreck where they had lived.
The fences rotted and fell to the ground;
And rank weeds grew upon the mellow loam
That they had broken up and tilled with care.

IV.

A CONTRAST.

A faithful people were deprived of homes.
There were no lands for them in the broad State
Of Texas; though upon the western prairies
Lay millions of acres of land untilled.
In early times these lands were surveyed out,
And tracks the most unreasonable in extent,
And most desirable, because they lay
In fertile valleys, cut by limpid streams,
Fell to the veterans of the Texan wars.
But railroad companies got most of it,
And they would not sell it at any price;
But held it, waiting for the settlers
To take up all the land around it.   Then
Its value would increase a hundred-fold.

And yet these people, lowly as they were,
Deserved as much as the old veterans.
Small children and fair damsels, blooming boys,
Young mothers and brave fathers had borne much
To open a way in the untried West,
And endured more to benefit the State
Than the adventurers who came to hunt,
And claimed a prior right to the rich soil,
And obtained patents on the finest lands.
In bravery, long-suffering, and toil,

They rivalled the heroes that stood the fire,
And laid down their lives at the Alamo.
Or those, with patriotic bravery,
Unexcelled in the annals of the world,
Who dashed upon the enemy at ease
On San Jacinto's ever famous field.

We all have read of the Acadian war;
And have grown tender-hearted as we thought
Of the hard treatment of those exiled ones;
And heaped imprecations on the heads
Of the oppressors and proud conquerors.
Great poets have taken them to be their theme,
And wrought of them highest harmonies,
And touched the softest chords of human love,
And asked for them the deepest sympathy.
But that was done in days of cruelty;
And war had long raged over all the land.

Here the most peaceful of inhabitants,
Protected by a peaceful government,
Were driven from their dwellings by the law
Held in the hands of tyrants, whose black hearts
If they were laid by Nero's, they would make,
By the contrast, his pure and white as lilies.

V.

THE CONSUMMATION.

That fall after the crops were gathered in,
And Mr. Warder moved to his new home,
And ease and plenty seemed thrown round their lives,
Lancium and Heclea were married.

There was no dazzling display of wealth:
None were invited but their long-tried friends.
The union was serenely beautiful,

As all things natural change with perfect ease ;
For it was a sweet joining of true love—
First love—and it seemed natural from the first
That they should be united for all times.

VI.

THE DROUTH.

The winter prior to the first dry year
Was very hard, with northers frequent and
Severe.   But little rain or snow fell throughout.
And the spring opened with gulf clouds at morn,
That floated over in black heavy masses,
Low-threatening, and oft came down in fogs.
But old men shook their heads and said these clouds
Were a sign of dry weather, for they broke
And cleared away ere noon, and the sun shone.
Sometimes light showers fell, that made the ground
Moist, so the farmers plowed and sowed their crops.
But the subsoil was dry from winter-drouth.
And, as the summer opened without rain,
The wheat and oats dried up to grainless chaff;
And the corn, as it got a start to grow,
The roots struck the dry soil and it withered up.
There was no harvest, no gathering in the fall;
And never had such gloomy prospects stared
The people of West Texas in the face,
For hitherto they had ne'er known of want.
They talked of the dark times continually,
Wore a care-worn expression of the face.

But in September fell abundant rains ;
The ground being warm the grass sprang from the
       roots ;
And cattle, sheep and horses became fat.
And a fine winter grain grew and matured.

The farmers sold their surplus stock, and bought
Seed-wheat and put in a large autumn crop.

But the winter was like the one before,
Devoid of rain and snow, but more severe.
And spring passed with light showers. Wheat burnt
    up.
The corn grew on to tasseling, but was
So weak and withered that it made no grain.

As in the first year of the drouth, the sky
Was mystical. A brazen shadowy smoke
Seemed smeared upon the vault above. At times
An atmosphere oppressive, with a haze
As of earthquakes, enveloped everything.
Now people lost all heart, they could not work.
Many took their families and left their homes,
And, with their teams, went east in quest of work.
But in the long run those fared best who stayed,
For sickness preyed upon those in the east,
And few families unbroken returned home;
While those who stayed were not reduced to want,
For again in the fall fell copious rains,
·And followed grass abundant, and the stock
Grew fat. And hope revived again.
Cows, with distended udders as in spring,
Came in the evening lowing to the pens.
And nearly all the farmers had fat beeves
They sold, and with the money purchased bread.

Two years without the garnering of grain
Had passed. The farmers had procured bread,
But many were in debt. Their surplus land
Was mortgaged; and many still owed for grain
Which they had planted, and brought no increase.
The third year the winter was still more severe,
But rain and snow fall; and fall wheat
Did well; and people hopeful, plowed
In mighty crops of every kind of grain;
And in the summer an unheard-of yield
Was gathered to the faithful farmers' homes.

VII.

AN HEIR OF TEXAS.

A man who claimed land by inheritance
Possessed rich lands in all parts of the State,
For it seemed that his father had received
These lands for services in Texas wars.
This man possessed a fertile tract of land
Near where the Warders lived; and when they were
Forced to give up their homes, he offered them
Fair terms, and long and easy payments,
If they would buy and settle on his land.
And Mr. Warder bought a home from him.
He sold his stock, and paid half down in cash,
And several years' time given for the rest.

When Lancium and Heclea were married
Lancium bought land from him on the same terms;
And all the wages he had hoarded up
He paid down in part-payment, and reserved
Enough to put up a nice residence.

Several years had passed since Mr. Warder and
Lancium had settled their new homes;
They had made payments regularly until
The years of drouth hung o'er them like a pall.
And this heir of much land all o'er the State
Had made them such fair promises throughout
That they believed when good crops came again
They would be able to redeem their homes.
But otherwise this sharper had devised.
They had made valuable improvements; put
In and well tilled extensive farms. But there
Was a fair promise of a bounteous crop.
He feared, should he delay, they would be free;
So he wrote them an urgent letter, stating:
Owing to many failures he had sustained,
He must have what remained due on their lands
In cash at once, as their time had expired,
Or an inevitable change would come.

Mr. Warder and Lancium went to town
Upon receipt of this, to see to it.
They talked with this man's lawyer, and there learned
That everything was ready for a suit.
Their only safety was in speedy payment.
He was landlord, and they were only tenants.
And they with other lawyers held converse;
He had his deeds recorded; they were good;
And they were at the mercy of their lord.

There was but one alternative now left
For Mr. Warder and Lancium: They would
Go to this man and try to treat with him.
As they returned from town they called on him.
I will not give the interview in full;
There was no poetry in that bad man's ways,
There was no romance in his wretched life.
They told him to wait till they sold their crops,
And they would pay him all that was still due.
And he said he wished that he could do this,
But circumstances which he could not rule
Made it so that there could be no reprieve;
That their crops and improvements would not pay
The damages he had sustained by them;
But, as an act of mercy, they might take
A portion of their crops when they moved off.

VIII.

PLAINS OF GRAIN.

When Lancium left Mr. Warder for his home,
He rode through a rich country, and the view
Was most magnificent, and it allured
Him to ride to one of the neighboring hills.
He saw a panorama unexcelled:
Fine houses stood upon the rolling plains,
Or nestled in the vales of winding streams,

And the whole was a plain of waving grain;
And he thanked all the parched months of drouth,
That he could now appreciate such views.
The wheat and oats were yellowing into ripeness,
And the corn, tasselling, swayed with every breeze.
What more could now the joyous farmer want?
Here was bread for his children, and the cows
Had just turned back upon their homeward graze;
And sheep were feeding on the dreamy hills;
And the young cotton, just cleaned with the hoe,
Bade fair to bring them luxuries of life,
And deck their ladies fair with jewels rare.

And Lancium beheld, dash down the road,
The fine carriage and team bearing the heir
Of so much land in this broad, fertile State.
And he, with heart o'ercome with melancholy,
Mixed with abhorrence and contempt, turned home.

IX.

THE WESTWARD MARCH.

As Lancium came to his cottage door
The sun was setting; mild, soft rays were laid
Across the yard and garden, and the flowers
Looked dreamy, as if welcoming repose.
He entered, and there was a glad sight there;
But he could not imbibe its sweetness then.
The languid odor of the rose was there;
His little girl, in noisy glee, was scattering
The petals.   Heclea a sweet bouquet
Of red rose and the yellow was fashioning,
And all the dignity of womanhood,
Fond aspirations of motherhood,
Were blended in the beauty of her face.
Sank Lancium into the easy-chair.
There was such an unusual quiet in his way

That Heclea looked at him.   There was
An unspeakably tired look upon his face.
Immediately she divined the cause :
She had expected, and was prepared
To meet it as a thing she was used to.
She moved softly to him and stroked his hair,
And kissed him lovingly upon the cheek.
" That cruel man has hurt your feelings, dear ; "
And there was an awakening in her voice,
And all his hopes of manhood rose again.
" I have known he would do this all the time.
He hates us, and would ruin us if he could.
But he cannot take me from you, my love :
Our lives, our ways, are made more sweet and grand
By his attempts to crush us from the earth.
And look at our little child : she is
More precious than his lands and piles of gold."

Lancium drew his wife to him and kissed her lips.
" Yes, our love is not within his power—
I would not give you for the wealth of worlds.
But we must go from here without delay ;
For summer is now in its youth, and we
Can move while it is pleasant summer-time,
And build a shelter ere the winter comes.
Where shall we go?   That is what weighs on me.
Shall we go farther west ?   I like it best,
But there is a dark prospect even there.
I could, out there, buy a rich tract of land
From the State, and get twenty or thirty years
To pay for it ; and might meet all the costs,
If no misfortunes should betide our way ;
But in that time no telling what may be ;
I am afraid I shall ne'er own a home."
" We will go farther west," she firmly said.
" I think our destiny is settled there—
To move in the advance and make the way
For the hosts that are steadily marching there.
But why do they treat us so cruelly ?
We have done them no harm, but much for them.

But, then, our ways are not their ways, our land
Is not like theirs; they understand us not,
And seem to hate our quiet, simple lives.
But there is yet an opening in the West—
Unsettled prairies and pure, limpid streams.
It is what we have known always, and we
Love it. We can be happy nowhere else."
And, with a light upon his face divine,
With resignation said, "Darling, we will go!

THE END.

www.ingramcontent.com/pod-product-compliance
Lightning Source LLC
Chambersburg PA
CBHW032017010726
47493CB00007B/2439